The P
Skinny

To Kate

Julie Sandilands (signature)

Julie Sandilands

First published in 2010 by Julie Sandilands
Published in 2011 by Purple Flame Books

Cover design by Tim Ryan ©

Graphic design by Sylvia Breslin ©
www.sylvanphotographics.co.uk

Printed and bound in Great Britain Inky Little Fingers
Paper manufactured from responsibly managed andsustainable
sources

To purchase a copy of this book please visit:
www.juliesandilands.com
e-mail:jules.sandilands@btopenworld.com

About the Author

Julie Sandilands is originally from Cheshire where she lived until 1997. After completing her B.Ed. (Hons) in Business and Information Technology, she spent three years in Botswana teaching in a large government secondary school in the capital, Gaborone. She moved to Scotland in 2000 and now lives in rural Fife, Scotland.

Acknowledgements

To Gillian whose constant encouragement and relentless ideas helped to take this story to places it might not otherwise have gone.

To Tim Ryan who kindly agreed to create the image for the book cover. Tim worked as an art teacher at Lotsane Secondary School, Palapye, Botswana between August 1997 and December 2000. The imagery in southern Africa had a profound effect on the illustrator. This is reflected in the cover showing a baobab tree, the African night sky, and the type face on the 'do it yourself' road signs publicising lodges and hotels, common on any road trip in Africa.

To all the amazing people I had the pleasure of working and living besides in Botswana.

The man walked up the steps and into the bright lights of the hotel foyer. The receptionist smiled at him as he handed over his passport.

'Dumela Rra, I hope you've had a good trip.' She gave him the swipe card for his room and shouted for the night porter.

'It's OK, I can manage,' he said, as he swung his bag over his shoulder and disappeared through the swing doors.

His room was on the second floor and looked out across the pool bar. After a cool shower, he poured himself a drink out of the mini bar and lay down on the bed. The air conditioning unit rattled away, blowing cool air across his skin. He closed his eyes, tired from the long drive.

When he awoke it was still dark. He shivered, stood up and turned off the air conditioning. The digital clock beside the bed read 1.45 am. He picked up the unfinished whiskey and pulled open the sliding doors that led onto the balcony. The night was warm and the sky clear. He stood and looked out across the hotel grounds. A familiar sound caught his attention. He leaned on the balcony, focusing his eyes in the direction of the noise. After a few moments, he could see someone swimming up and down in the pool. He stared as the body glided through the water.

After completing several more laps, the person climbed out of the pool. At first he could only make out the outline. As his vision sharpened, his eyes followed the smooth contour of her body, unspoilt by any garments. He watched as she picked up her towel, wrapping it around herself, before disappearing from view into the darkness of the hotel gardens.

Chapter One

The morning sun was rising in the eastern sky, slowly covering the earth with a rusty glow. The air had a stillness about it as if in anticipation of the unfolding of a new day. It was already twenty-two degrees and not yet six o'clock. Abbey had never been a morning person and getting out of bed had always proved to be a chore, regardless of the time of year. That, however, had been twelve thousand kilometres away in Manchester, England. That was where Abbey had been born, schooled and spent the first thirty-two years of her life. Here in Kasane, Botswana, the dawning of a new day heralded the start of another adventure just waiting to be experienced.

She rose with ease and dressed into cargo pants and a long-sleeved shirt. The heat and mosquitoes were difficult adversaries and Abbey knew better than to try and ward them off by state of mind only, as malaria was a very real threat in this part of the country. She pulled on her walking boots, after having held them upside down and banging them together to dislodge any insects that might have crept in during the night. Substantial boots were also a necessity if scorpion bites were to be avoided whilst walking through the bush.

She left the small bungalow and made her way down to the bottom of the hill towards the village to buy fresh milk and bread. There were no pavements anywhere in Kasane and, apart from the main road in and out of the town, which was tarmac, the remaining roads were simply well-used dust tracks.

Goats, dogs, donkeys and chickens roamed freely around the town. The goats wore collars with bells that jingled constantly, and being woken up at five in the morning, when their day began, had taken some getting used to. The rickety, corrugated iron shops were already open, selling anything from electrical items to vegetables.

The smell of barbequed corn wafted through the air. Music thumped out of a cassette player and many of the locals were also up and about on bicycles, or on foot, making their way to work. Children, immaculately dressed in their blue and white uniforms, made their way to the local community junior school, waving and shouting to people in cars and trucks as they drove past.

Kasane lies adjacent to the Chobe/Zambezi River and is the most northerly town in Botswana. The charity, African Volunteers Project (AVP), had been active here for many decades. Abbey had joined the forestry unit, helping to plant new saplings and educate the locals on how to look after the newly-planted trees.

The land had been protected as a non-hunting area for some decades and eventually declared as a national park. As a result, the ever-growing elephant population had reached immense proportions as herds had flocked from the surrounding countries of Namibia and Angola for the safe haven of the Chobe Park and the thousands of acres of bush land, south of the river, down to the Okavango swamps. The daily damage to the bush land was now threatening other species of wildlife. Trees could not be planted fast enough, and keeping them safe from being trampled or eaten by these enormous, ravenous mammals was proving to be a far greater task than ever expected.

Abbey entered the local Spar shop, her t-shirt already sticking to her from the heat. She bought what she needed, practising her limited Setswana to the delight of Beauty who worked in the shop. Abbey had been impressed by the welcome she had received from the local people and their attitude towards foreign, white people coming to live and work in their country. She suddenly understood what it meant to be in the minority, and wondered if the ethnic minorities back home felt as comfortable as she did as she wandered freely around, familiarising herself with the town and its inhabitants. She was also impressed with the standard of English spoken by the

8

majority of people, who would never miss an opportunity to stop her on the street and try out their language skills.

There were many stalls of various shapes and sizes selling the most obscure and random items, yet this was the only shop made from bricks and mortar with an electric till which offered a good selection of groceries and household goods.

The temperature was rising fast as Abbey stood outside the shop. She smiled and breathed in the clean, dry air, surveying her new world with ever-increasing wonder.

Chapter Two

Four months previously on a late August, Sunday afternoon, Abbey had been sitting in front of her computer, staring vacantly at the screen. She was working on her personal development plan as her annual appraisal was scheduled for the coming week. Abbey worked for a printing firm in the heart of Manchester, working her way up from office junior to the marketing director. She had dedicated her life to her career and was a valued and respected member of the firm. It had, however, been a difficult week for Abbey, involving a dispute over whose job it was to look after a couple of international clients. It had always been her responsibility and she had been shocked to hear that the Costello account was being given to one of her less experienced colleagues. Abbey had questioned the decision with Colin Trump, the Managing Director, and demanded a meeting in his office.

'Abbey, we think that the Costello account would be better off with Nigel at the moment.'

'But Mr Trump, I've looked after that account for the past five years,' Abbey had protested.

'Exactly dear,' smiled Mr Trump, 'and we think it's time for a new approach, which we believe will benefit us all.'

Abbey knew exactly what he meant. A change of approach would ensure the clients wouldn't be lost. Was she losing her touch, or her mind?

'Abbey,' continued Mr Trump, 'you're scheduled for an appraisal next week. It might be an idea to start working on your personal development plan in preparation for that review.'

Targets and objectives for the future seemed to evade her and she decided that a strong cup of coffee might help. She leaned on the kitchen worktop, gazing out into the garden. It was approaching the end of the summer and the flowers and bushes were in full bloom. She was in no doubt that 'Nigel' wasn't suffering from the same mental block and was probably planning his takeover strategy for her job!

Frustrated, she started to look through *The Independent* newspaper she had bought earlier that day. She skipped the first few pages before scanning the TV and entertainment guide. She continued to flick over the pages until she reached the employment section. Abbey often did this on a Sunday to see if any of her company's competitors were advertising similar positions to the one she held. She decided there was nothing of interest and was about to fold away the paper, when she spotted an advert. It was the opening line, in big, bold letters, which caught her attention.

OUR OBJECTIVES ARE CLEAR – ARE YOURS?

Abbey read the advert. The charity, AVP, was looking for volunteers to work on an environmental rejuvenation project in the north of Botswana. Intrigued at what this might entail, she looked up the charity's website and read about the programmes currently in progress. The organisation welcomed applications from people from all walks of life, who were willing to offer their time and skills in parts of the world that still relied on the support of international agencies. AVP's main objective was to provide training and education to the native people to maintain their own environment in the long term, and for future generations.

After reading the advert in the newspaper, she had thought about what skills she could offer, and was confident that the sheer determination she possessed in all aspects of her life was a good enough start for any volunteer. She was intelligent, quick to learn and had good people skills. She opened the newspaper and read the advert again. She pictured the forthcoming appraisal in her head.

'What objectives have you for the coming year, Abbey?' Mr Trump would ask, peering across the desk at her. 'And how do they fit in with the Company Plan?'

11

What would she reply? Ah yes. 'Well sir, I'd like to develop my...'

What *would* she like to develop? What sort of challenge would she like to see land on her desk? She mulled it over, her thoughts jumping from one dimension to another. It was true that Abbey had complained at her last appraisal that she felt she was not being developed, and her job no longer provided any real challenges for her. Maybe, she thought, this idea to try something different was an inner yearning to break free from the monotonous routine she had inadvertently created for herself. Whatever it was, it resulted in a major life-changing decision for six weeks later in the middle of October, she had boarded a British Airways flight at Heathrow heading for Gaborone Airport.

She had officially requested the time off at her appraisal, and Mr Trump and the HR Manager (after checking company policy several times), had reluctantly agreed her request for an unpaid career break for one year.

The reaction from her colleagues had been mixed, ranging from her being totally mad, to pangs of jealously from people who either didn't have the financial resources, or the courage, to step off their own treadmill and venture out into the unknown. Had Abbey given herself time to think her plan through, her rational thoughts might have saved her! However, she had not and, with a packed suitcase of fashionable clothes, shoes and makeup, all of which would become totally redundant in the months to come, she boarded the aircraft with a sense of trepidation and excitement.

That is why Abbey Harris was buying breakfast supplies at six-thirty in the morning in the bustling, rural town of Kasane. By eight o'clock she had finished her breakfast and had arrived at the tiny AVP office in the west end of the town. Richard was already there sitting at his desk, feet up and sucking the end of his biro.

'Morning,' he said without looking up.

Richard had been at Kasane for a full six months before Abbey had arrived, and used this opportunity to establish himself as the 'team leader', much to Abbey's amusement. After their first week of working together, she had established that Richard was about as capable of making good quality decisions as the monkeys, who screeched their way through the day in the trees.

'Morning Richard,' she replied. 'You're bright and early this morning. Couldn't sleep? Or is there something important I need to know about?'

Richard looked up from his paper and studied Abbey before answering. He had always found over-confident women frustratingly annoying and Abbey was probably the worst he had ever met.

'No, my dear,' he said, knowing the sentiment would rasp on her nerves. 'I just thought I'd get up to speed with all the paperwork before we head off this morning.'

Abbey didn't respond as she knew that, after an hour's overtime the day before, there was no outstanding paperwork. There never was. She was far too efficient for that and Richard knew that too.

Richard was in his late forties and an ex-school teacher from Cumbria. He had been the head of the technical department and reluctantly taken early retirement on health grounds. *More likely pushed* thought Abbey, as she looked at the day's work schedule.

'Oh, I see we're due at the primary school this morning to talk to second years.'

'Ah yes, I thought I'd do that given my previous experience with children, Abbey. I would like you to go and collect the new delivery of saplings from the Crossroads.'

'I thought you said you were going to go this week?' she queried.

'Like I said, I think it best if *I* do the school visits. Don't you?'

Abbey smiled at Richard's idea of himself as the patron saint of all children. The same children who called him bush names that were quite derogatory, but very funny. She thought it was his bushy beard and the occasional snorting sound he made when he laughed, that the children had picked up on.

13

'Fine with me, I'll take the bakkie.' She picked up the keys to the Toyota pickup and left, more than happy to spend the morning on the open road.

Abbey pulled over at the last small house going out of the town. She pushed the wrought iron gate, which whined as it swung open, walked up the path over-grown with weeds, and tried the front door. As expected, it opened with one push.

'Phil,' she shouted. 'Phil, are you up yet?'

The living room looked as though it had been the scene of a riot the night before. Dirty clothes, overflowing ashtrays and empty beer cans covered the floor. Phil was the third member of the AVP team and had arrived the same time as Abbey. He had become as much a friend to her as he was a colleague, and a close bond had quickly developed between them.

He appeared at his bedroom door, wearing nothing but his boxers. His tousled, mousy-coloured hair fell over his face partially covering his eyes. His chin was dark with stubble, as it usually was, and he looked as if he hadn't shaved for at least two or three days.

'Morning sleepy head,' said Abbey, looking at his tall, slim frame.

'What time is it? You're a bit early, aren't you?'

'Is that your way of saying thanks for coming to pick you up? Not to mention covering for you with Tricky Dickey!' she replied, clearing a pathway across the floor with her foot.

'What? Did he ask where I was?'

'No, but I suppose I didn't give him the chance. I left the office as soon as I had my orders. Anyway, where have you been exactly?'

Phil groaned a reply and disappeared back into the bedroom.

Ten minutes later they were on the road, Phil eating two fat cakes he bought from one of the makeshift stalls by the roadside. A fat cake, or 'Magwinya', was like a heavy doughnut and a staple part of the African diet. Phil stuffed both of them into his mouth at once. He smiled at Abbey, who shook her head at his lack of etiquette.

'Great for hangovers, these things,' he muffled, his mouth full.

'You stink,' she replied, screwing up her face and opening her window.

'Thanks Abbey, I can always depend on you to say what's on your mind.'

Abbey smiled and continued to drive, avoiding the livestock that had wandered onto the road.

Phil had settled into African life very easily, spending most of his spare time in the local bars or shebeens in the town. Alcoholism was rife in small, rural, African communities, where people had too much time on their hands, sitting in the shade out of the heat in the middle of day and drinking cold beers. Unfortunately, this usually carried on until the early hours of the morning and Phil had often arrived late to the office, smelling like a brewery.

He was fifteen years younger than Richard, who had decided to promote himself as a fatherly role model. He had taken Phil to one side and given him a talking to about the perils of drinking and local women. Much amused, Phil had nodded his head vigorously and thanked Richard for his advice. Abbey had tried to slide under the desk to hide her laughter. Richard, however, had just smiled at Phil, patted him on the back and called him 'son'. That had done it, and she couldn't contain herself any longer. She had left the office, shouting her excuses and walked home.

'Where are we going then, hun?' asked Phil, winding down his window to let in the warm breeze as they left the town and headed south.

'Still alive then are we?' muttered Abbey sarcastically.

'Oh Abbey, don't be like that. You know you're turning into an old spinster more and more each day.'

Ouch, that hurt. Yes, she was single now, but Abbey had been married before, to her teenage sweetheart from school. They had married at eighteen and divorced exactly one year later, when it suddenly dawned on both of them that they actually had very little in common. She had managed a few relationships since, but none of

15

them had lasted more than about three months, as the limited conversation and predictable sex they offered failed to satisfy her on both levels. Here she was, at thirty-two, chastising a guy the same age as her for being reckless.

'I'm sorry,' she said quietly, taking a deep sigh. 'I guess I've forgotten how to party.'

'That, my dear, is easily remedied,' laughed Phil, swigging back a can of coke.

'Anyway,' continued Abbey, 'we've been instructed to pick up the new saplings whilst teacher Richard does the chat with the primary school kids.'

'Fine,' Phil nodded. 'I thought he wanted to do it this week?'

'That's what I said too, but hey I'm not going to argue.'

Abbey smiled to herself. Being out in the bush with Phil, stinking or not, was much better than a morning listening to the same rehearsed speech she had heard more times than she cared to remember.

The Crossroads was exactly fifty kilometres south of Kasane on the main Francistown road. It consisted of a café and a car park. It was a popular meeting place and the transfer of goods tended to take place there. There was really only one main road in Botswana, which went from Gaborone, the capital, up the east side of the country right into the heart of the Chobe National Park. It was straight, long and notorious for accidents as people either fell asleep at the wheel, or crashed trying to avoid wildlife, which would appear on the road without any warning. There were very few stopping places from Francistown to Chobe, and the Crossroads Café provided a welcome stop for travellers in need of a coffee and a break from the road.

Abbey looked at her watch. It was still only ten o'clock in the morning and the delivery of saplings usually arrived between eleven and twelve. This would give them time for a coffee and a chat with Isaac, who ran the café bar.

Isaac greeted them both and welcomed them as long lost friends, even though it had only been a week since they were last there. Isaac was one of the tallest men Abbey had ever met. His hair had turned pure white and he always wore a friendly smile, revealing an immaculate set of teeth. He had crossed the border with Botswana from Bulawayo in Zimbabwe about twenty years ago and, despite not having an Omang identity card, he had always managed to escape arrest from living and working as an illegal immigrant.

'Two coffees please, Isaac,' called Abbey as she made her way over to a table by the window.

'Yes Mma.'

Abbey handed over a twenty-pula note, which was enough to cover the coffee and a tip. Isaac spoke perfect English and sat and chattered with them both whilst the café was quiet. He was genuinely interested in their work and what they were doing and Abbey thought he would make an excellent addition to the team. Had he been in Botswana legally, she would have certainly approached Richard with the idea.

Isaac was also renowned for his homemade beef burgers sourced from the succulent, organic, local cattle, and they were now part of the fixed Wednesday routine as much as the collection of the trees.

'A quarter pounder and a double cheese burger please, Isaac,' shouted Phil.

'A double, Phil?' said Abbey, aghast. 'You've just munched on two fat cakes, which are akin to lead weights!'

'Look hun, got to keep my strength up. Don't know what the rest of the day has in store for us now, do we?' He smiled at a couple of burly Afrikaans who sat at the next table. 'Got an insatiable appetite this one!' he said, pointing at Abbey, a mischievous smirk on his face.

Abbey shifted uncomfortably in her chair and smiled sarcastically back at him across the table.

By midday, the bakkie was loaded with new trees and they were on their way back to the office. Richard was already there when

17

they arrived. He studied Phil carefully to try and detect any sign of a hangover.

'Got everything?' he enquired.

'Everything,' replied Abbey, already writing up the new stock numbers in the purchase book.

After unloading the trees off the bakkie, the rest of the day involved walking around the new plantation not far from Abbey's house, checking that the newly installed irrigation system was working properly.

'So, what are your plans for tonight?' asked Phil, as he cleaned the end of one of the plastic pipes.

'Usual,' replied Abbey.

'Oh, that'll be bath, bed and a date with Agatha Christie then!' chuckled Phil.

Abbey smiled. Despite Phil stomping with his size nines once again on sensitive ground, she couldn't help but like him.

'Going to make me a better offer then, stud?' she said, looking directly at him.

Abbey had never viewed Phil as a potential dating opportunity, and had never imagined being intimate with him in any way, but she enjoyed his company immensely. Plus, he had a wicked sense of humour and made her laugh. That in itself was worth a couple of hours of her time.

'Well, as it happens,' he replied, 'there's a short shorts do at the President's Lodge tonight. Heard the chat about it last night in the bar. Fancy going?'

There were two safari lodges in Kasane. The President's Lodge and the Savuti Lodge. The Savuti Lodge was the more upmarket lodge of the two and much more expensive. The President's Lodge was not quite as exclusive and was used by locals, tourists and Dutch men wearing particularly short, khaki-coloured shorts, shouting drinks orders in their guttural Afrikaan tone.

The hotel stood about fifty metres from the riverbank, giving easy access to the water safaris and fishing trips regularly organised

18

by the hotel guides. Around the main building lay approximately ten acres of immaculately tended grounds, abundant with trees, shrubs and brightly coloured flowers. The furnishings were of good quality and the hotel boasted a swimming pool, two restaurants and a hairdresser, who was housed in a tree house in the gardens not far from the river. Customer service was second to none, and Abbey had compared their attitude and willingness to help as far superior to any experience she remembered having back home.

In a bid to escape the heat during the hottest months, Abbey had sneaked into the pool at the President's Lodge in the very early hours on several occasions, and swam naked in the refreshing, cool, clear water under the moonlight, with nobody but the bullfrogs and the crickets to keep her company.

She thought for a minute. 'Yeah, OK. I'll meet you there?'

'Smashing. See you about eight in the terrace bar.'

'See you there - and Phil,' she called after him, 'don't be late.'

He smiled and, with a wave of his hand, disappeared down the hill.

Chapter Three

Abbey arrived at the Lodge at exactly eight o'clock. She walked through the beautifully kept gardens, carefully keeping to the path so as not to tread on the delicate flowers and shrubs. As predicted, Phil was nowhere to be seen. The last time she had been at the hotel had been a couple of Fridays ago during the notorious happy hour. Alcohol was cheap enough in Botswana, and getting an order of four double gin & tonics for the equivalent of a few pounds provided any serious drinker with the challenge of drinking them before the ice melted.

She had sat at the bar with another ex-pat from Birmingham, Judith, who had a temporary contract teaching in the local junior school. A rotund, partially bald South African had approached them and attempted to make conversation, focusing most of his attention on Abbey. His name was Mr Permelo and he was the manager of the Savuti Safari Lodge. He had lived in Chobe for several years and his reputation for being an intimidating, self-opinionated bully was well known. Abbey found it amusing that he would rather drink in this bar than his own, even though everyone knew who he was, and very often avoided him.

As the evening wore on, she had felt particularly uneasy as his arm slowly wound its way around her waist.

'How is business at the Savuti?' she had asked, trying to move away from his roving arm.

'Just finish your gin and tonics, girl,' he hissed down her ear. 'Then we'll go back to your place and make some business of our own.' He clasped his hand tightly around her wrist, his hot breath on her cheek.

Abbey had quickly excused herself to the ladies and walked straight out the front door of the Lodge and back home. She had sent a message to her friend via the doorman that she had left the building. Ever since that evening, Mr Permelo had made no attempt to communicate or acknowledge Abbey in any way, which had come as great relief to her as she still shuddered with disgust at the mere thought of him getting close to her.

Phil arrived within minutes of her finding a table on the terrace bar overlooking the pool. She saw him approach, still looking slightly dishevelled, but wearing clean jeans and a typically boyish grin.

'Hi hun, been here long?' he asked, as he sat down opposite her.

'Not really. I got you a Castle, that OK?'

'Perfect,' he smiled. 'Cheers!'

'So what's this in aid of then?' Abbey asked, looking around at the ever-growing crowd.

'Oh,' replied Phil, 'it's in recognition for enterprise and for local businesses in providing employment.'

The tourist industry was thriving in Botswana, and wealthy businessmen, mainly from South Africa, had been quick to settle here and take advantage of the droves of visitors, predominately Americans, hoping to get a glimpse of the 'big five' on safari and were willing to pay big bucks for the privilege.

Abbey had noticed that the increased injection of wealth into the local economy was not being filtered down amongst all the towns' inhabitants, with wages remaining appallingly low; the divide between those who had and those who had not was constantly growing and very evident. Local housing usually consisted of the typical rondavals or simple, oblong, breezeblock buildings divided into a living room and a bedroom where the whole family slept. This was a far cry from the ex pat community and some of the wealthier locals who lived in much larger bungalows, with running water, electricity and a maids' quarters at the bottom of the garden.

Phil leaned towards her and said in a low voice, 'Don't look now but there's a guy over there that keeps looking over here, and I don't think it's me who's caught his attention!'

'That is so damned annoying, Phil. Don't look now but! When can I look then?' she whispered impatiently.

'No need, he's walking towards us.'

As the man passed, Abbey's eyes followed him. He was tall, slim, with tanned skin and fair hair. He stopped at the bar and turned around just in time to catch her as she surveyed him. He smiled to himself and turned back to face the bar.

'Damn,' she said through gritted teeth. 'I don't believe that. He just caught me looking at him. God, this is so embarrassing!'

Phil sat back in his chair, looking very bemused at Abbey. 'You really don't get out much, do you?'

'What do you mean by that?'

'Look hun, most of these events are just cattle markets, a free for all. Most of the wives are left at home to tend to the kids, if you get my meaning?'

Yes, she did get his meaning, which didn't actually make her feel any less uncomfortable. She felt the sudden urge to leave but, before she could move, the man walked over to their table.

'Hi,' he said, offering his hand first to Phil and then to Abbey. 'My name's Darren. I'm pretty new around here and you two don't look either like tourists or members of the Afrikaans Mutual Appreciation Society!' He spoke with a soft English accent, and Abbey immediately noticed his piercing blue eyes.

After the initial introductions it was Phil who started the conversation.

'Want to join us?' Phil motioned to the empty chair next to Abbey.

Darren nodded and sat down, careful not to brush Abbey's legs as he squeezed past.

'What you doing in Kasane, Darren?' asked Phil.

'I'm a prospector. I've been given a four-month contract to prospect a two hundred kilometre area. As there is slightly more in the way of human activity around here, I thought it would be a good place to base myself.'

Botswana, like other African countries, was rich in diamonds and relied on them as the main source of revenue into the country. The Botswana Government was a substantial shareholder in an international diamond company, which had complete control over the sourcing, excavation, and distribution of diamonds from Botswana onto the market. It provided vital employment in many areas and was the principal benefactor in the improvement of Botswana's infrastructure. Once a prospecting license had been granted to assess a certain area, prospecting companies were employed to carry out initial exploration to assess the viability of a full dig.

'Isn't that a bit of a risky career?' asked Abbey, who had been reading articles about blood diamonds and human rights abuses in some of the other African countries.

'I guess it could be anywhere else,' replied Darren, picking up on her line of thought. 'The Botswana Government has got the whole situation completely sewn up. If they hadn't, I wouldn't even think about working here. The foreseeable future of this country relies on the income generated by diamonds. If they go down the route of some of their neighbours – well, let's just say that the Botswana we're currently enjoying will no longer exist. There's just too much to lose, for everybody.'

As the evening wore on, Abbey felt much more relaxed and lost the initial embarrassment she had felt when he first approached. They both found Darren very easy to talk to and the conversation flowed as each of them talked about their work and life in the heat and dust of the African bush.

'Have you been to Kasane before?' enquired Abbey.

'Twice,' replied Darren. 'Only for a couple of days at a time though. I usually stay here at the Lodge. Do you still come here to swim, Abbey?'

Abbey froze on her chair. Mortified at his question, she felt her cheeks burn with colour. Now feeling extremely uncomfortable, she used the next opportunity she could to leave.

'Well guys, I'm really tired. I have to work in the morning, so I guess I'll turn in.'

Darren stood as she rose from her seat. Phil looked over at her with an incredulous look on his face, which she tried not to notice. She bid them both good night and left for the comfort and privacy of her own home, her cheeks turning scarlet each time she thought about his question.

Perhaps she should have answered and said, 'No, sorry, you must be mistaken, Mr Scott. I've never swam here, ever!' However, Abbey had never been good at telling lies, not even little white ones. Her tendency to blush always gave her away.

The next morning, Phil was already sitting at his desk when she arrived at the office.

'Well, this is a first!' she exclaimed sarcastically. 'Have you been to bed?'

'Not desperate for a shag then?' said Phil, continuing to read his paper without looking up.

'Excuse me! What do you mean by that?' she rebuffed, shocked at his comment.

'You last night, Miss Frosty Knickers. That guy Darren was just about drooling and then you decide to leave!'

'Look Phil, not everyone wants to jump into bed with someone within five minutes of meeting them, you know. Don't put me on your desperate level. Anyway, there was more to it than that.'

'Like what?'

'Nothing, really - now just drop it, will you?'

Phil didn't reply, but shrugged his shoulders and left the office to work outside. Abbey had never told Phil about her skinny-dipping and knew he would howl with laughter if she explained her embarrassment at Darren's question.

Later that day, Abbey was walking to the Spar shop when she spotted Darren leaning on his bakkie, talking to the manager of the President's Lodge on the other side of the road. She held back, using

24

the opportunity to look at him more closely. She guessed he was in his mid thirties. He was reasonably attractive and she had noticed his strong, muscular arms the night before. Abbey had always found muscular arms attractive in a man. Perhaps it was a sign of his ability to keep hold of her, she wasn't sure; but skinny arms were a real turn off, despite the fact that muscular arms tended to be joined to broad, strong shoulders... She made her way quickly into the shop and waited for him to drive away before leaving.

The week passed and Abbey and Phil's relationship hadn't suffered any damage, although Abbey's love life was certainly not the topic of conversation again. The new saplings had been planted with the help of a band of volunteers from the town. Education was as important as the planting of new trees. It was imperative that locals continued to plant and care for young saplings long after AVP had left, if the National Park was to thrive in the long term.

Abbey enjoyed this aspect of her work and tended to do the more practical training out in the bush, leaving the classroom work to Richard. Despite the heat, she loved getting her hands dirty and wore her hair scrapped back in a ponytail. This was a far cry from the Abbey who had left Manchester a few months before. Immaculately manicured nails, make-up and stylish designer clothes had been Abbey's stamp, and she was always careful never to be seen looking any other way.

At the end of the afternoon shift, she would walk home through the bush, taking care to keep to the allotted pathways. Wild animals were part of bush life and respecting their space and their nature helped to avoid any unwelcome attacks. Occasionally, some of the lionesses wandered into town in the night to steal the odd goat, but rangers were always on hand and arrived in plenty of time to usher the beasts back before anyone or thing ended up on the menu.

Abbey had been given a small brick bungalow at the top of a path which wound its way out of the town, and into the mouth of the bush. The house was moderately furnished, but provided the bare essentials and, after a good clean, and her personal effects scattered about, she felt quite at home. It consisted of two bedrooms, lounge, kitchen and a bathroom.

Across the front of the house was a wooden veranda with a swing bench. As time passed, Abbey spent more time out here than she did inside. She had become used to recycling her bath and washing-up water to keep her plants watered and viewed water as a precious resource, something that had never occurred to her in England. It now seemed sensible to her that the national currency was called 'pula', the Setswana word for rain.

Although crime was not a problem in the town, Abbey had learned the hard way that keeping doors, windows and fly-screens shut when the house was empty was essential. The Park was inundated with monkeys who did not recognise any boundaries, and viewed all property as free game. They were small, light-brownish in colour and amazingly agile, very noisy and could squeeze through a slightly ajar window with ease. Abbey had only been in Kasane a couple of days when she returned from work to find the house trashed, and most of her underwear and fridge contents strewn about her garden. The monkeys had sat in the nearby trees watching her tidying up, screeching across the trees tops to one another.

Phil had laughed when she told him the next day, as Abbey had previously described the monkeys as cute and funny, and had argued this point with Richard when he used a sling shot to frighten them away from the office.

'I hope you're going to admit to Uncle Richard that he was right and you were wrong!' Phil had teased. Abbey had decided not to mention the episode to Richard at all, and begged Phil not to either.

The bungalow sat in approximately half an acre of land and was encircled by a three-foot, interwoven metal fence, which was covered in pink and red rhododendrons. In the middle of the garden stood a large Marula tree; the sturdy branches provided the perfect haven for weaverbirds to build their nests in. This tree housed several nests, and Abbey would sit for hours watching the small, yellow birds fly in and out of the tree, armed with dry grasses and twigs.

The nests were dome-shaped and always built by the males. She had been amused to hear that the female weaverbird would inspect the finished nest and the male would wait for her approval on a nearby branch. If the nest was not approved, the female would destroy it and the process would start all over again. There was absolutely no question which gender was in charge in the weaverbird world!

As well as learning about the African culture on a daily basis, she was also learning about the other inhabitants that wandered freely in and out of her house and garden. Abbey had been sweeping the front porch when she encountered her first baboon spider. This type of spider was quite common and closely resembled it cousin, the tarantula which, to Abbey, just meant very large and hairy!

The spider had walked fearlessly past her as she stood, frozen on the spot, broom in hand, waiting for the imminent attack. It stopped, sensing her presence, before scurrying down the steps and under the house. She had decided that these particular spiders were far worse than the flat, crab-like ones that hid in dark closets and cupboards, clinging to the walls, and moving rapidly sidewards once the door was opened. Even now, they never failed to make her jump each time one scuttled out of sight. At home in Manchester, the appearance of a spider in the house usually resulted in a full-scale operation which included neighbours and, on one occasion, a passer-by walking down the street. By Abbey's standards, she thought she was coping extremely well.

She was, however, decidedly worried about what might be living under the house, as she had seen various animals and insects taking refuge under there. One rather large, brown, furry animal regularly ran under there when Abbey opened the garden gate in the afternoon. Phil had suggested it might be a mongoose which, according to him, was good, as mongooses killed snakes. He advised Abbey to leave it be. Whatever it was, underneath the house was certainly a place she would never dare to venture and find out.

Lizards of various sizes were also regular visitors to the bungalow, sunning themselves on the porch. These did not worry her at all as they kept the insect population down, and that, thought Abbey, could only be a good thing! Fortunately, she had not yet had a visit from any monitor lizards, which looked like small crocodiles and lived by the riverbanks.

Darkness fell across Botswana just before seven o'clock in the evening all year round. Abbey spent the long, warm evenings sitting on the veranda, observing the amazing starry skies, and listening to the rhythmic trill of the crickets. Her favourite time to sit out on the porch was when it rained. She found the sound of the raindrops falling steadily onto the dry ground comforting, as it lifted the blanket of heat and cleared the dust and humidity. Once the rain had retreated, it was followed by a flurry of activity from animals and insects, as if they had tasks that had to be completed in record time.

In all, Abbey's new lifestyle created ample opportunities for her to sit quietly for long periods of time. This was a totally new concept to Abbey who, in the past, had usually only sat down long enough to down a Latte in Starbucks during her lunch break, if she bothered to take one. Abbey had finally learned to relax and enjoy the moment in time, rather than continuously thinking about the next. She thought about her job with AVP; despite it not being high profile or well paid, it had given her a sense of satisfaction that had eluded her in the past.

This thinking time had also allowed her to review the past and clear her head of memories that played over and over again in her mind. She hadn't necessarily blamed herself for the breakup of her marriage, but she knew that all the blame couldn't be laid at her ex-husband's door. They had been young, naive and, if she hadn't had been in such a rush to force her independence by leaving home, the situation might have been quite different.

It felt good to mull over past events and, in some ways, bring closure and a release of the guilt she had felt over letting other people down. In fact, she had concluded that the decision to take time out from her life had been a good one, and so far had no regrets.

Chapter Four

Over the next couple of weeks, Abbey saw Darren around town on numerous occasions. Sometimes, she managed to avoid being seen, and other times it was a quick smile and a wave as Darren's bakkie passed her. She had noticed that he hardly ever seemed to walk anywhere and, much to her relief, she had never seen him in a pair of short shorts! He had rented a small house about five minutes drive from the centre of town, and appeared to live alone. Abbey also noticed his bakkie parked outside the Spar shop occasionally, which caused her to reconsider where she bought her groceries from.

She chastised herself for being so childish. What was the matter with her? Was it so bad that he had seen her swimming in the dead of night, naked? It wasn't that she didn't like him - or maybe that was the problem? Maybe she *did* like him and she was worried that he didn't like her, or at least not enough to create an opportunity to ask her out. She laughed at herself. Maybe she was over analysing the whole thing.

The situation was soon put to the test as she walked home that Friday afternoon. Darren's dark green bakkie was parked outside the Spar and, although Abbey had enough milk to last until the morning, she walked through the door and over to the counter. Darren was standing with his back to her, looking at the wine bottles. She picked up a litre of milk and went to pay Beauty at the till.

'Dumela Mma, glad it's weekend?' chattered Beauty.

'As always, Beauty. What about you? Have you any plans?'

'Oh, I gotta work as usual. Got no choice there. Too many mouths to feed!'

'Hello again,' came the familiar voice behind her.

Abbey turned and smiled.

'Hi,' she replied, feeling her cheeks burning yet again. 'How's the job going? Settling in OK?'

They walked out of the shop together as he answered both of her questions. There was a short, uncomfortable silence before he bid her goodbye and drove away. She smiled at her stupidity. No, he wasn't interested in her at all. *Good*, she thought, *what a relief!* It would make things much easier in the future. No more looking around corners to check the coast was clear, although skinny-dipping at the lodge was definitely off the agenda from now on. As she walked home her heart wasn't entirely flowing with the same sentiments as her head.

When she arrived at her front door there was a visitor waiting for her on the swing bench. Abbey smiled and waved.

'Hi Judith, I've been meaning to call you. I've not seen you about for ages. Where've you been?'

'I've been in Palapye, covering for a teacher who's been off with suspected malaria,' replied Judith. 'I only got back this afternoon. So what's new, anything?'

Abbey shook her head. 'No, not really,' she replied, wondering if she should report the latest arrival in town. 'Anyway, I want to apologise.'

'Really! What for?'

'For leaving you high and dry the other week in the President's Lodge. Remember, at the happy hour?'

'Oh, god yes, I'd forgotten about that. It's OK, I guessed what had happened. He's some toad that guy, isn't he?' giggled Judith. 'I have to say, though, he didn't have any interest in carrying on whatever the conversation was with me. Guess I'm not his type!' She started to laugh heartily, holding on to her hips.

Judith was in her mid fifties and what the Africans would describe as traditionally built. Her hair had greyed and, when she laughed, she held the attention of everyone within half a kilometre, as the sound filled the room. She had befriended Abbey straight away, popping around for tea and going out socially to the lodges for a drink. Phil had never accompanied them on these nights out, making any excuse he could think of, and Abbey had detected a hint of disappointment on Judith's face when she turned up alone.

They spent a pleasant evening swapping tales. Abbey cooked stir-fried vegetables and they ate on the veranda, surrounded by citrus candles to ward away the mosquitoes. By the time Judith left to go home, Abbey was feeling quite tipsy. She fell into bed and slept soundly. She awoke early the following morning, her dream still fresh in her mind. She had been hiding behind a bush in the President's Lodge gardens watching Darren swim naked in the pool. He had got out of the pool, smiled and waved at her, knowing she was there all the time. She had run all the way home as fast as she could, not daring to look back.

The following Wednesday, Richard had gone to the junior school to talk about the importance of tree rooting and compost. Phil and Abbey were back on the road to pick up the next delivery of saplings. The delivery still hadn't arrived by one o'clock, and was now well over an hour late. Phil and Abbey were not particularly bothered and quite happily munched their way through beef burgers and chips under the cool ceiling fans in the café.

'Do you think we should continue to wait?' Abbey asked Phil as he ordered a second portion of chips.

'Well, we can't leave now,' he replied still eating. 'That guy drives for over four hours to get here. I think he'll be pretty pissed off if we've given up on him and he has to drive all the way back, complete with the load he left with.'

Abbey nodded. Yes, Phil was right and she would just have to ring Richard on the landline at the office and explain. Richard wasn't back from the school and the answer phone clicked in. After leaving a message that they would be back much later than usual, Abbey had the distinct feeling that Richard would not take this news well and half expected a row when they got back. He would just have to like it or lump it. There was nothing else to be done. At least she would have time to rehearse her defence speech on the way back.

When Abbey returned to the table, Phil was chatting to a man Abbey recognised from Kasane.

'Hey Abbey,' said Phil, 'this is Mr Kobe, from the Savuti.'

Mr Kobe was the assistant manager at the Savuti Lodge and, compared to Mr Permelo, was a breath of fresh air. He was renowned for his hospitality and always gave his guests a warm welcome whilst never compromising his professionalism when socialising in the town. Abbey smiled and shook his hand. Mr Kobe smiled and lowered his head.

'Anyway, Mr Kobe has been on a training course in Francistown,' continued Phil. 'He's seen our guy down there and apparently the truck's broken down. It's being fixed and he doesn't reckon he'll be here until six!'

'Yes,' nodded Mr Kobe looking at Abbey. 'He knew I would see you here and asked me to pass on the message. He would like you to wait.'

'Thank you. I appreciate you taking the time out of your day to do this,' said Abbey, before turning to face Phil. 'Shit, now what do we do?' she groaned. 'You know it will take us at least an hour to load the trees, and it'll be dark by then and that road is lethal by day, let alone by night.'

'Miss Abbey,' said Isaac who had been listening in to the conversation. 'You know I have room here and I would be happy for you both to stay and leave early in the morning. I think it would be much safer.'

Isaac leaned on the counter, his huge hands spanning across the wood. The noise of Phil clearing his throat made her turn to look at him. Phil's grin couldn't have been any wider as he nodded encouragingly at Abbey to accept the offer.

'Is there enough room for us all?' asked Abbey.

'It is fine. I will sleep in the café tonight.'

Abbey looked again at Phil and then at Isaac. 'Oh, OK. I don't suppose we've got much choice really. Thanks Isaac, if you're sure it's no trouble?'

'You are never any trouble Miss Abbey,' he replied, grinning.

Before Abbey could speak, Phil had returned to the counter and ordered two cold beers, which soon turned into four and then six. The trees arrived just after six and, with the help of Isaac and some other customers who were persuaded to help with the promise of a beer and a cigarette, the bakkie was loaded in just over half an hour.

Abbey and Phil resumed their spot in the café and settled in for a pleasant evening. Phil showed off his skill at playing pool, confidently beating both Isaac and Abbey almost effortlessly, taking twenty pula off each of them. After her fourth beer, Abbey was feeling totally relaxed and made herself comfortable over a couple of chairs.

'Phil,' she said. 'You know that guy Darren we were talking to the other week at the President's Lodge?'

'You mean that guy who made you blush, twice?'

'I don't remember that bit,' laughed Abbey defensively. 'Well anyway, did you and he stay on after I'd left?'

'Yeah, we were there until midnight.'

'Did he say anything about a girlfriend anywhere, I mean...'

'Hey, I know what you mean,' laughed Phil interrupting her. 'No, he didn't mention any girlfriend, or wife for that matter. All I know is that he's taken a six-month lease out on the old Fernella house just out of town, and I think he said his family comes from Bath. He did mention he has an older brother who lives in Christchurch, New Zealand with his wife and kids. Apparently, his father died a couple of years ago and his mother wasn't coping living alone so, she went to live with the brother to help look after him and his family. Oh yeah, and he did a Geology degree at Newcastle.'

'Hmm,' Abbey nodded. 'You found out quite a lot considering.'

'Let's just say I have a friend who I thought might be interested!'

'Why didn't you tell me all this before then?' asked Abbey.

'Because you made it very clear to me, when you bit my head off the next morning, Miss Frosty Knickers, that you weren't interested in him.'

'No, Phil, if you remember rightly I said I wasn't interested in bedding him within five minutes of meeting him. I never said I wasn't interested in him! Not that I am, obviously,' continued Abbey, looking sheepishly into her glass.

Phil rolled his eyeballs and shook his head. 'Women, Isaac. I'll never work them out!'

Isaac took full advantage of their company that evening and hung up his apron to join them on the other side of the counter. He entertained them with stories about the customers that had used the café over the years, some of whom included locals from Kasane and, more often than not, Phil had stories of his own to supplement Isaac's. When Abbey felt her eyes becoming heavy, she excused herself to bed, not realising it had only just turned nine o'clock.

Using a torch, she made her way to the small wooden shack at the back of the café. She breathed a sigh of relief when she stepped inside as the house was clean and tidy, and not what she had expected from a bachelor living on his own. She hoped Phil might take a leaf out of Isaac's book and decided she would mention it to him before they left the next day. Isaac had already put two sleeping bags out, one on the floor and one on his bed. Abbey smiled at his thoughtfulness, hoping the one on the bed was for her and not for Phil. She decided that it didn't really matter, as that was where she was going to sleep!

Early the next morning, after being force-fed breakfast by Isaac, they said their goodbyes and were on their way back north. They chatted idly about their evening when Phil brought up the subject of Richard, and what he would say to them when they got back. Abbey had to wipe away the tears as Phil did an impression of Richard, demanding to know where they had been, and what had taken them so long.

'It was a simple errand, even the monkeys would have managed.' He imitated Richard's voice perfectly, snorting in between words, which Richard often did if he was laughing or angry. 'You know that guy gives me the creeps,' shuddered Phil. 'Give him a pointy hat and a fishing rod and he'd pass for a garden gnome any day.'

Phil took his eyes off the road momentarily to look at Abbey, joining in with her laughter, when the look of horror on her face made him look back at the road. A young bull elephant had suddenly appeared out of the bush, running out in front of them. Phil tried to swerve, but the truck skidded. It overturned and landed on its roof, down a ditch on the side of the road.

Although it had happened very fast, Abbey knew she had not lost consciousness. She looked over at Phil in the driver's seat. Both of them had not been wearing seat belts and Phil's head had hit the windscreen. The glass had shattered. His face was badly cut and blood was trickling down his chin, and also from a deep cut on his scalp. His eyes were closed.

'Phil! PHIL! For god's sake, talk to me,' shouted Abbey.

Phil groaned a reply, much to Abbey's relief and she started to try and release herself from the cab. The door was jammed tightly shut. She knocked out the rest of the broken glass and crawled out of the open window. Kneeling on the ground, she reached for her mobile phone from her shorts pocket, but it had been thrown from the truck when it overturned. Frantically, she scanned the parched ground looking for it.

'Phil, I can't find my phone,' she shouted, as she ran her hand across the grass.

'Use mine,' cried Phil from the bakkie.

Abbey made her way around to the driver's door, took the phone from Phil's shirt pocket and wiped the blood off the small screen.

'Shit, no signal. Can you believe it?' Abbey looked around her, trying to establish exactly where they were. The heat shimmered as she looked down the tarmac road. 'Phil, can you move at all? Do you think you can get out of there?'

Abbey was now concerned that the truck might blow at any time, as petrol was starting to spill out of the tank onto the dry, brown grass. She knelt beside the driver's door and tried to wrench it open. The cut on her knee stung as it took the weight of her body as she leaned forward, pulling on the door with all her might.

'It's no good Phil, I can't move it,' she cried, trying to stop the panic she was feeling rising in her voice. Tears of frustration welled up in her eyes as she made yet another attempt to move the twisted metal. The noise of an engine made her turn. Darren's bakkie was coming along the other side of the road from the direction of Kasane. He swerved over to them and parked behind the overturned truck. In no time at all, he had powered the door open and was checking Phil's pulse.

'How long ago did this happen?' he said, without looking at Abbey.

'Oh, I don't know... I'm not sure. Maybe about five minutes ago. I... er...'

'OK, let's try to get him out and into the back seat of my truck. I'll drive closer, and Abbey, keep him talking.'

'Do you think it's OK to move him?' she asked quietly.

'Abbey! For Christ's sake,' wheezed Phil, his body bent awkwardly over the steering wheel. 'Just get me the hell out of here, will you?'

Between them, they managed to slide Phil out of the crumpled truck and into the back of the twin cab. She half turned in her seat, asking him questions to keep him awake. In what seemed an eternity they eventually arrived at Kasane Clinic.

Abbey sat patiently on the bed whilst the nurse cleaned the cut to her forehead and bandaged her right hand and her left knee, which had needed two stitches. She also had a nasty bump on the top of her head where she had hit the roof of the bakkie as it had overturned. Her headache was slowly starting to ease after taking the pain killers the doctor had prescribed.

Richard had been in to see them both, but had left after half an hour, complaining of feeling queasy at the smell of disinfectant, and the fact that hospitals always made him feel ill.

'Can I go and see Phil now?' she asked the nurse.

The nurse nodded. 'Yes, see your friend, he's being a baby. Can you hear him? See if you can keep him quiet!'

Abbey followed the sounds of the pathetic yelps down the corridor and into the room where Phil was lying on the bed. The nurses were treating his cuts and bruises. An x-ray had shown three broken ribs and he needed stitches to the cut on his head.

'Hi,' said Abbey, as she popped her head around the door. 'Want me to hold your hand while you have your stitches put in?'

Phil smiled back. 'God, it's good to see you. Are you OK?'

'I'm in a much better state than you!' she replied. 'That was a close one, Phil. I thought the truck was going to blow and you were a gonna. I really did. If Darren hadn't shown up when he did...' she paused, 'well, I don't know what I'd have done.'

'I think you'd have managed perfectly well.'

Abbey turned. Darren was stood in the doorway.

'Hey, thanks mate,' said Phil, smiling at Darren, as he made his way over to the bed. 'I owe you big time, and yeah Abbey was as cool as a cucumber as I remember. In fact, hun, you can join me in a crisis anytime!'

Phil smiled at Abbey, who he thought looked decidedly embarrassed at Darren's arrival and also that her face looked slightly flushed. They both sat by Phil's bed until the nurse invited them to leave. Phil was being kept in overnight to make sure there was no internal bleeding.

'Oh god,' gasped Abbey. 'I've forgotten about the bakkie. It's still on the road!'

'Don't worry, it's all been sorted,' replied Darren. 'My lads brought it back in. It's write-off though, so I've left it with Moses down at the garage. We unloaded the trees that could be saved at AVP and I told your boss where the bakkie was before I came here. Come on, I'll give you a lift home.'

They travelled the short distance up to the bungalow in silence. He helped her out of the bakkie by taking her hand. They walked up the wooden steps to the front door.

'Thanks for everything today,' said Abbey quietly. 'I really do appreciate what you've done.'

'You were lucky I was around. I was on my way to a meeting just south of Kasane. I must drive up and down that road about ten times a day at the moment! Anyway, I'm sure you'd have done exactly the same for me.'

He leaned forward and kissed her on the cheek, his hand gently holding her chin. 'Goodnight Abbey, I'll look in on you tomorrow.'

She watched the truck as it disappeared out of sight. Abbey went into the dark bungalow and stood with her back against the door. Without any warning, she burst into tears and sank to the floor.

Chapter Five

Richard left the small clinic and made his way down the main street towards the Savuti Lodge. He stopped at the garage to look over the crumpled wreckage of the bakkie.

'That's the problem with that woman,' he tutted under his breath. 'She always thinks she knows best.' He walked around the truck, his mind penning the damming letter to head office, complaining about Abbey's complete lack of responsibility and respect for charity property. Ah yes, he knew exactly what he would say.

Mr Permelo was waiting for him in the small casino at the lodge. Richard made his apologies for being late, relaying what had happened.

Mr Permelo smiled and shook his head. 'You know you need to bring that woman under control, Richard. She has ideas above her station, that one.'

Richard nodded in agreement.

'If you need any ideas,' continued Mr Permelo, 'I'm quite happy to help.'

'I might just take you up on that,' replied Richard, waving at the bar tender to refill the glasses.

Richard and Mr Permelo met on the same day and at the same time every week. Richard had acquainted himself with Mr Permelo not long after he had arrived to work for AVP. He had been impressed with the South African's direct attitude with his staff and noticed, when he shouted orders, people literally jumped to attention. That was Richard's way too. He had had that authority in the classroom and hadn't been afraid to use it. He had found managing the AVP office very frustrating and, at times, futile. Phil, he had decided, had never jumped to attention in his life. His laid-back attitude grated on Richard's nerves and that woman, well… Mr Permelo had a very valid point as far as she was concerned.

It wasn't long before the bar quietened down and the two men could talk about the business they had met to discuss.

'I've two girls who think they want to be waitresses,' said Mr Permelo quietly. 'One is a local girl and the other is from Mahalapye, here to live with her aunt.' Richard nodded and Mr Permelo continued. 'I'll send the girl from Mahalapye round tomorrow. Usual routine.'

It had been on one of their first meetings that Mr Permelo had brought up the subject of Richard living on his own. Richard had agreed that, although it wasn't an ideal situation, it was better than living with a woman who either didn't know her place, or couldn't string an intelligent sentence together. Mr Permelo had been delighted to come up with a solution that would benefit them both.

'I get lots of casual labourers looking for work,' explained Mr Permelo. 'I don't have the time for them. I'm too busy running this hotel. If I do need staff, there are plenty of Kaffirs I can call on. What I could do is send the girls to you for an 'interview' and trial run for, maybe, a week. The job description is purely down to you, Richard, but I think it could cover all your needs. Of course, if you think one might be good enough to work here for me, I would consider it, after a good reference from you of course.'

Richard had smiled and given his approval. It sounded like an ideal solution. 'What can I offer in return?' he had asked.

'I need plants and trees for the hotel gardens. They're difficult to source and not cheap to buy. I'm sure AVP wouldn't miss a few now and again!'

'I'm sure that won't be a problem,' smiled Richard.

The usual routine was that the hopeful applicants would go to Richards's house at four in the afternoon when he had returned from work. The arrangement had worked extremely well and, after the promise of a good reference to Mr Permelo, all his needs had indeed been met. He left the bar happy with the prospect of female company over the next week. However, there was another female on his mind who he needed to attend to first thing in the morning.

Chapter Six

Abbey was woken by the sound of knocking on her front door. As she lay for a second or two, the knock turned into a constant thump. She rolled out of bed and flinched at the stiffness of her muscles as she made her way across the floor. She opened the door. Richard was standing there, looking very annoyed.

'I thought you'd be up by now, Abbey,' he chastised. 'It's gone eight thirty!'

'What can I do for you, Richard?' yawned Abbey, as she put the kettle onto the stove.

'Aren't you coming into work today?'

She turned to face him. 'Richard, it may have escaped your notice, but I was in a road accident yesterday and I could have died! I have a cut on my face, my hand is still sore and I feel like shit. So no, I will not be coming into work today. What I *will* be doing, is visiting my friend and colleague who has also been injured and is probably still in hospital. Now, would you like a cup of coffee whilst your here?'

'No coffee thank you, and it didn't escape my notice that you had been in an accident given the pickup is completely written off. I hope AVP are insured, that's all I can say. What you were thinking of staying out all night, I'll never know.'

'Look Richard, I made an executive decision, OK? I decided that, as the truck from Francistown was definitely on its way up the road, we had better wait for it. I also decided that it would be far safer to drive back in daylight rather than in the pitch black.'

'Hmm, well I'm not sure your last executive decision was the right one. Do you?'

Abbey stayed silent and kept her back towards him for fear of throwing the kettle at him.

'I better go,' said Richard, breaking the silence. 'Someone's got to keep the home fires burning, as they say. I'll see you tomorrow?'

'You might - you might not,' hissed Abbey through gritted teeth.

The fly screen banged against the frame and Richard muttered something indecipherable under his breath as he stomped away down the hill. Abbey took a deep breath and shook her head at his insensitivity and lack of compassion

'What a total arse,' she muttered to herself. 'Typical friggin school teacher. Always right, always got to have the last bloody word.'

She made her way back to bed, holding a cup of coffee in her left hand.

Phil was at home and lying on the sofa when she arrived at his house later that afternoon.

'Is that wise?' she asked, pointing at the empty beer cans already stacking up on the table.

'Purely medicinal,' replied Phil, taking another slurp.

'Did you manage to carry them over here yourself, given you have broken ribs?'

'Nah, paid one of the kids five pula. Now he keeps coming back every ten minutes to check whether I need another delivery!'

Abbey cleared a space on a chair before sitting down, and relayed the visit she'd received from Richard earlier that morning.

'Well,' said Phil. 'It's gonna be at least a week before I'm back, and old Rickcardo can stick that up his proverbial. Honestly, what is his bloody problem with the rest of the human race? Hey, do you think he's married or has been?'

'Hmm, not sure,' shuddered Abbey. 'He's not the easiest person to talk to, is he? And he doesn't exactly have any animal magnetism. At least not that I've noticed.' She looked at Phil and smiled. 'Anyway, you behave yourself, OK? Otherwise I'll be sending Nurse Judith round to tend to your broken body!'

'Steady on now, hun,' laughed Phil, clutching his ribs. 'Don't go putting images into my head I really don't want there.'

Satisfied that Phil was alright and on the mend, she left the bungalow and walked home. Children were playing barefoot on the road, rolling old car tyres with sticks. She smiled at the pure simplicity of an activity that brought so much pleasure, that didn't have a complicated instruction manual or cost a fortune. The children recognised her from school visits and shouted 'hello' as she walked past. She smiled and waved back at them. She had just turned to walk up the hill when Darren pulled up beside her.

'Hop in,' he said, 'I'll give you a lift up the road.'

Abbey happily accepted and climbed gingerly into the cab.

'I told you I'd look in on you today. How you doing?'

'I'm feeling a lot better thanks. Just a bit sore and I've got bruises in the most peculiar places.' She rubbed her shoulder as she spoke.

He smiled at her and pulled up by the porch steps. 'I have something that belongs to you. The guys found it when they brought the truck in.' He handed a mobile phone to her.

'Wow, thanks. At least now I still have all my contact numbers, assuming the damn thing still works.'

'It does,' he replied. 'I took the liberty of checking it for you.'

'I'll put the kettle on,' she said when they got inside. Darren smirked at her. 'What's so funny about that?' she asked, slightly bemused at the expression on his face.

'It's not so funny, as so British!'

'I'd make you something to eat as well, but I haven't been shopping and this hand is still quite sore and…'

Darren held his hand up and mouthed 'stop' at her. Without another word, he went out to the truck and appeared with two plastic bags full of shopping.

'I'd already thought of that,' he said, 'so I came prepared. Now, do as you're told, sit down and I'll pour you a glass of wine.'

Darren busied himself in the kitchen. He listened intently as Abbey chatted about her job with AVP, and the antics her and Phil had managed to get up to since they arrived. She explained why they had stayed the night at the café and then decided to set off early the next day to try and appease Richard's mood.

'I feel a bit of a fool actually,' she said. 'There I was thinking I was being sensible and avoiding a possible accident by waiting until daylight. Some good it did us!'

'Listen, don't be so hard on yourself. We both know there have been literally hundreds of accidents on that road over the years, some a lot more serious than yours!'

'Thanks,' Abbey smiled. 'Unfortunately that's not quite how Richard sees it. You'd think he was going to have to pay for the repairs out of his own money!'

They spent the rest of the evening swapping stories about past jobs and the current delights of working outdoors. She sat beside him on the sofa, taking note of his soft features and toned body. He seemed to sense Abbey's scrutiny and leaned over to fill her wine glass, brushing her hand with his in the process. He smelt divine, of soap and a hint of cologne and, still feeling slightly vulnerable after the accident, she could have quite happily sunk into his arms there and then.

It was midnight when Darren stood up to leave. She walked with him to the door.

'I seem to be thanking you quite a lot at the moment,' she smiled, looking up into his blue eyes.

'Don't worry, I'm writing out IOU's on a daily basis now,' he laughed. 'See you soon, Abbey, and take care of yourself.'

This time he put both his hands on the base of her neck, kissing her on the forehead before walking away into the night.

Chapter Seven

After a week of rest and recovery, both Phil and Abbey were back at work. Phil still had the yellow smudges of bruises on his face, but his spirits were high and he was back to his usual self.

Abbey had not seen Darren since their dinner at her house and she hadn't seen him around town either. Not that she had been specifically looking for him of course, or that she really had time to think about where he was.

Two government ministers from Gaborone were going to visit in a couple of days on a promotional tour before the up and coming local elections. The town had been preparing itself for the visit and banners and flags had been hung on buildings and fences. School children were going to be given the day off to line the main road and cheer the ministers as they drove past and the local choir had been practising for days.

Richard was frantic, as they were visiting every organisation that promoted Botswana in a positive light, and AVP was one of them. He was busy writing up a plan that included a tour around some of the plantation sites, and a speech with a photo opportunity right outside the office.

'They'll have journalists following them everywhere,' he said, going over his plan for the seventh time. He looked up at Phil. 'You'll need new trousers.'

'What?' replied Phil, in a higher-pitched voice than normal. 'What's wrong with shorts and a t-shirt, Richard? Aren't we supposed to look as if we're hard at work?'

'Some people work hard and dress smartly at the same time,' he retorted.

Phil tutted under his breath, threw his pen onto the desk and walked out of the office.

'Well, that went well,' smirked Abbey. 'The diplomatic core certainly missed out on you, Richard.'

'Hmm, and you're not much better.'

Abbey whooped with laughter as Richard followed Phil out of the door. She muttered 'dick' when she thought he was out of earshot.

The day of the visit arrived. Richard had Phil and Abbey standing to attention outside the office, waiting for the cascade of black cars to pull up. They both looked clean and smart. Richard was pacing up and down in front of them. Abbey felt like she was back at school in assembly on a uniform inspection day.

Phil leaned over and whispered in her ear. 'Seen anything of lover boy?'

'He's not my lover!'

'Not yet.'

'Phil, I'm warning you. Let's not go there, unless you want us to fall out and I'll make a scene in front of our nice visitors,' she said, still smiling and barely moving her lips.

'Oooh, tetchy today, aren't we? OK, OK, don't look at me like that. I promise I won't mention Darren or the word 'lover' ever again, at least not in the *same* sentence anyway. Oh look, is that Darren's bakkie that's just pulled up over there?'

Abbey craned her neck to look in the direction Phil was pointing, when she realised she had fallen straight for his wind-up.

'Phil, all I am going to say is that you are incredibly immature sometimes. Therefore, I am going to treat that childish attempt at a joke with the contempt it deserves.'

'Tetchy.'

Before Abbey could reply, the cars arrived and several men wearing dark suits and sunglasses descended onto the AVP plot.

Richard's rehearsed speeches were applauded and Abbey kept herself busy by offering glasses of fruit juice to anyone nearby. Phil, she noticed, had disappeared for a brief spell, reappearing by the shed at the top of the first plantation, pretending to look very busy with a spade, just as the cortège prepared to leave. Despite all the worrying Richard had done, the visit went smoothly and to plan, leaving the three of them with a sense of satisfaction as they watched the cars drive away in the direction of the church.

That evening the government ministers were hosting a pre-electoral ball at the Savuti Safari Lodge. It included a five-course dinner and the invitation stated 'formal dress required'.

'I'm not going,' said Phil, throwing the invitation onto the desk. 'I don't do formal dress - never have, and never will.'

'Listen cowboy,' panicked Abbey. 'You've got to go. Otherwise, I will be left in the company of our esteemed team leader and you wouldn't do that to me, would you? PHIL! Would you? Hey, do you want me to go down on my knees or something here?'

Phil looked up, ginning like a cheeky school boy. 'OK then. But I'm ditching early if it's crap.'

It wasn't until she had got home that Abbey remembered that she hadn't done formal dress for a while either. She looked in the mirror at her reflection. Her hair was clean but hadn't been cut or shaped for months. Her blond highlights had started to grow out and she frowned at the darker colour now coming through. She scrutinised her face. It was covered in freckles from the sun and, being fair-skinned, it had made them even more prominent.

After a warm shower, Abbey took out the suitcase from under her bed that still housed the clothes she had brought with her, and which she felt represented another life entirely. An hour later she left the house with her hair elegantly arranged on the top of her head, three-inch heels, and wearing a Pierre Cardin black dress, which flattered her figure and defined her curves.

She arrived at the hotel fifteen minutes late on purpose. The plan had worked and both Richard and Phil were already standing in the reception area, drinking champagne. As Abbey walked towards them, Phil's mouth dropped slightly.

'My God, Abbey. Never seen you spruced up. Looking good, gal!'

Abbey smiled. 'Thanks Phil, you're looking rather dashing yourself tonight.'

Phil returned the smile. He *had* made an effort and was wearing dark trousers and a white shirt, which looked as though the iron may have skimmed over it in a few places. They turned, looked at Richard, paused, and said nothing.

The usual mixture of businessmen and women had been invited and jostled for an opportunity to speak to the politicians, who were surrounded by security men. Mr Permelo was on manager's duty and Abbey caught him staring at her on more than one occasion. His loud voice carried across the room making his presence very predominant. She shuddered and was determined to keep as much distance from him during the evening as she possibly could.

Abbey, Phil and Richard mixed with the crowds, making polite small talk, before moving into the dining room. Each table was covered with a white, silk tablecloth with a small, colourful flower arrangement in the middle. Bottles of red and chilled white wine stood ready on the table, and it was obvious that this was a 'no expense spared' evening. A band hired for the occasion played popular music on the stage. Waiters and waitresses stood at each table, white-ironed cloths draped over their arms, ready to take orders

'Just going to the ladies, Phil,' said Abbey, as they made their way towards the table with 'AVP' written on a card in the middle. 'Save me a seat, next to you!'

Abbey made her way to the main reception and was just about to turn left into the ladies' toilets when she saw Darren walking up the steps to the main door. She stood momentarily, trying to decide whether to run into the toilets or go and greet him. It was too late to run. He saw her, smiled, and greeted her with a peck on the cheek. As he did so he whispered, 'You look stunning Abbey, you really do.'

Abbey smiled but felt her cheeks go flaming red as she tried to avoid looking directly back at him. Darren was wearing black jeans with a cream-coloured linen shirt that complimented his tanned arms. *Hmm, not quite formal*, thought Abbey, *but delicious all the same*. Not caring about Richard's reaction, she invited Darren to join them at their dinner table, and he willingly accepted.

Phil was in excellent form as the free champagne and beer started to infiltrate his blood stream, and began to sing his own version of the Tom Jones' hit 'It's not unusual' as loudly as he could so as not to be drowned out by the band, which were playing the song in tune. Richard, after giving Abbey dirty looks for inviting Darren into the company, was more relaxed than Abbey had ever seen him, happily tapping his feet to the music.

The evening went by pleasantly enough and, by two o'clock in the morning and after the umpteenth yawn, Abbey decided it was time to go home.

'I'll walk you back,' offered Darren. 'I'm not driving tonight as I knew I would end up having a drink.'

'Were you going to walk home?' asked Abbey.

'Actually, I have a room booked at the President's Lodge. So it's not a problem to walk you back, as I'm going in that direction.'

They left the noise of the ongoing party and headed towards the bungalow. Nobody was about and, apart from a solitary dog barking behind one of the small shacks, it was silent. Darren took Abbey's arm and linked his own through it. The stars shone magnificently in the dark, African sky, lighting up the path in front of them.

'Have you enjoyed yourself tonight?' asked Darren, as they approached the house.

'Very much,' replied Abbey. 'Apart from my feet, which are in excruciating pain from wearing these damned shoes.'

In an instant, Darren scooped her up into his arms and carried her the last ten metres to the house, setting her down gently on the porch. Giggling, she took his hand and led him to the swing bench on the veranda. They sat in silence in the darkness, her head resting on his shoulder. He held onto her hand, stroking it gently with his thumb. She pulled up her knees and let them fall onto his lap.

'Whoops, I'm forgetting my manners,' she hiccupped. 'Would you like coffee?'

'No thanks.'

'Tea?'

'No thanks. Abbey...'

'Beer?'

Before she could reel off any more refreshments, he took her face in his hands and kissed her lips. He tasted as delicious as he looked and she responded by putting her arms around him, pulling him in tight against her body. His fingers moved tenderly across her shoulders, down her arms and round the bottom of her back. He lifted her once again and carried her into the bungalow. She closed her eyes and prayed that the rest of the night would be anything but predictable.

Chapter Eight

Abbey awoke to the smell of coffee on the bedside table. Darren was already out of bed and getting dressed.

'Morning,' he whispered, walking over to the bed. 'How are you?'

'Oh, I'm... I'm just great,' she smiled, reaching out and pulling him on top of her.

'Hey, I'm sorry but I've got to go to work today,' he said. 'In fact, I should have been there over an hour ago!'

'What? It's Saturday!'

'I know, but being self-employed means you go to work whenever you need to, and I need to go today. If you want to come with me you're more than welcome, and it would definitely make the day much more bearable.'

'OK, I'll come along, but do we have to go right now?' she whispered, sliding her hands up the outside of his thighs, feeling the firm flesh underneath the loosely-wrapped towel around his waist. 'Right this very minute?'

The relationship between Abbey and Darren grew stronger each day. They were regularly seen out together and his bakkie was usually parked outside her house in an evening. Phil teased her intolerably at work about being able to foresee her future even if she couldn't. She smiled at his jokes and comments, as she felt more content now than she had done in a very long time, and knew that secretly Phil was happy for her too.

The only down point, as far as Abbey could see, was that the longer distance jobs kept Darren away for up to a week at a time and, although they had only been together for a relatively short space of time, she missed him terribly when he was away.

Judith, on hearing the good news, had turned up at the AVP office, demanding to know every last detail about Darren from the day they had met. Abbey described their first meeting at the President's Lodge and Phil repeatedly interrupted her with his own version of events. It was only when Abbey offered to go to the shop to buy cakes, leaving Phil to entertain Judith, that he fell silent and offered to run the errand himself.

One stifling hot, Wednesday morning, Abbey walked down to the office after saying goodbye to Darren, who was going to be away until the weekend. Both Richard and Phil were already there. Richard had his head deep in a memo from Head Office and Phil was tapping his biro on an empty glass.

'Morning guys,' she said breezily, helping herself to a glass of water before sitting behind her desk.

'Morning as in good morning, because I don't happen to think it is, or morning as in just morning?' Phil said in a contemptuous voice.

'OK, grumpy guts, what's biting you then?'

'Ask him,' replied Phil, pointing over at Richard with his pen.

Abbey looked over at Richard. 'Well Richard, anything the matter?'

'No, no, not at all,' Richard replied. 'I've had a memo from Head Office to say they want us to go on a team-building day to improve communication, and I have to organise it. That's all, nothing major.'

Nothing major! A team-building day with Richard and Phil! *Oh my god*, thought Abbey. The only building her and Phil had ever done, as a team, was to build a tower of empty beer cans, balancing a vodka bottle on the top as high as they could before it fell down. How they had laughed when it crashed onto the floor.

'Maybe we should discuss this collegiately, as a team, given it's about team building?' suggested Abbey. 'What do you think, Phil?'

Abbey looked over at Phil who had his head under the desk and seemed to be searching for something on the floor. 'Phil, what are you looking for?'

'Oh, just some enthusiasm,' he sniggered. 'I'm sure I can find some down here if I look hard enough!'

Ignoring Phil's guffaws from under the desk, she turned back to Richard. 'Have you got anything in mind?'

'No, not yet, but leave it with me. I'm sure I can come up with something special.'

Abbey cringed at the thought of Richard's 'something special'. Should she be honest here and tell Richard she had organised more team-building days than she had fingers to count on, and maybe she could do it for him! No, she decided against it and thought she would let him wear his brain cells out instead.

Two days later, Richard arrived early at the office wearing a newly-pressed white shirt, knee-length khaki-coloured shorts and thick, knee-length, white socks. His protruding tummy (or muffin top, as Abbey described it), hung over the thick leather belt around his waist. Abbey pointedly refused to look at Phil to avoid any fits of the giggles at Richard's attire.

At ten o'clock, he marched Phil and Abbey down to the edge of the Chobe River.

'OK guys, today's the day. This is our team-building day,' announced Richard. 'I have everything we need,' he said, pointing to the rucksack on his back. 'Full packed-lunch for everyone! Nothing spared.'

Abbey looked around and then at Phil, shrugging her shoulders.

'Right, here he is,' continued Richard. A young man was walking towards them. 'This is Mopele, everyone, and he's going to be our anchorman today, if you'll pardon the pun!'

Phil rolled his eyeballs, which Richard ignored and carried on talking. 'Mopele is going to lend us his transport today.'

'Richard, I'm sorry, but I can't take the tension anymore. Will you please just get to the bloody point?' said Abbey impatiently, fanning her face with her hat.

Richard took a deep breath. 'Today, for our team-building activity, we are going to travel down the river by boat, together.' He grinned at the pair of them, a hint of excitement in his voice.

'Excellent,' said Phil, suddenly finding some enthusiasm. 'I've never been on the Chobe Fish Eagle Safari Steamer before. Wow, far out Richard!'

'Er no, not the Fish Eagle Phil,' said Richard, a little amused at the suggestion. 'Mopele has kindly agreed to let us take his boat for the day.'

At Richard's signal, Mopele went over to a pile of bush wood and pulled out a makoro.

'So, they've asked you to organise a team-building day with no budget,' said Phil. 'Great, bloody marvellous.'

'Well, I certainly didn't pay for the sandwiches,' retorted Richard.

'Richard,' fired back Phil, 'for a start that is not a sodding boat. It's a tree trunk with a big hole in the middle. Secondly, are you aware how hungry the hippos are at this time of the year? And thirdly, what the hell is wrong with the Fish Eagle's comfy seats and fully-stocked bar?' He pointed towards the double-decked steamer moored on the jetty.

'Well, this is a great start,' said Richard, now sounding very annoyed. 'I have put a lot of thought into this and I am not going to change my plans now. Mopele, put the boat into the water.'

Phil walked over to the makoro once it was in the water, and noticed it already had a puddle of water forming on the floor.

'Not watertight, not safe, not going,' he announced firmly, looking at Abbey and pointing to the deepening pool in the bottom.

'Are you refusing to take part in this activity? Because if you are, you leave me no choice but to report this to Head Office,' spat

Richard, incensed at their lack of cooperation and appreciation for all his hard work.

'No, I am not refusing Richard,' replied Phil. 'I am just saying that I have serious concerns about the whole safety aspect of this. However, if you are prepared to go over to the other side of the river and return in one piece, I will think about - no, I will gladly - join in.'

Without a word, rucksack still on his back, Richard stomped over to the water and climbed precariously into the makoro. He took the paddle and pushed away from the bank. The makoro weaved into the water and, within seconds, the back end started to dip. Richard, realising he was sinking, shouted over to Mopele for help. Abbey turned around just in time to see Mopele walking with speed back towards the town, a fifty-pula note sticking out of his hand.

'Richard, get back here now, before you drown!' shouted Abbey, trying to control her voice.

Richard paddled furiously back towards them. About a metre away from the riverbank, the makoro disappeared under the water and Richard, totally drenched, crawled back onto dry land on all fours. Abbey and Phil were both bent double, shaking with laughter.

'Are you alright?' spluttered Abbey, reaching out her hand to help him stand on his own two feet. He ignored her offer of help. Instead, he hauled himself to his feet and stormed off back towards the office, the rucksack trailing on the ground behind him, which attracted the attention of a troop of monkeys who could smell soggy, wet sandwiches in the near vicinity. They congregated into little groups and followed him as he walked up the road, making high-pitched screeches in excitement, as the distance between them and their lunch narrowed.

'Well, what now?' asked Abbey, tears streaming down her cheeks.

Phil, in no better state of control to the point where he couldn't speak, pointed over to the Chobe Fish Eagle, which was boarding a group of tourists for the next trip.

An hour later, Phil and Abbey were comfortably entrenched on a bench seat on the top deck of the steamer, sailing down the Chobe River with their second double gin and tonic.

'I know,' said Abbey standing up, glass in hand. 'Let's play spot the hungry hippo,' and she pointed to a family of hippos bathing quite happily in the cool water.

They both crumbled into a heap as they laughed, going over Richard's ungracious landing. 'Actually,' continued Abbey, 'I read that hippos don't eat humans, they just kill them if they find them in the water.'

'Well hun, that's something I don't ever want to put to the test.'

The river cruise wound its way down the river, Zambia on one side and Botswana on the other. Above them was an immenseness of pale blue, which stretched as far as the eye could see. Wispy clouds created a latticework across the sky.

Herds of elephants waded out into the river, totally ignoring the steamer as it gently chugged its way through the reeds and the water. Baby elephants followed their mothers, struggling to keep up as the water got deeper. They trumpeted loudly as they drank and cooled themselves, using their huge trunks to squirt the river water across their backs. Crocodiles slithered back onto dry land, camouflaging themselves against fallen logs, waiting patiently for the next hapless victim to stumble on their paths.

The top of the steamer was uncovered and the relentless sun beat down on them.

'You know,' said Abbey, draining her glass. 'We really should do this more often.'

'What, get pissed on the riverboat?' chuckled Phil.

'No! Do the tourist thing. I've really enjoyed today and there is so much of the Park I haven't seen yet. Honestly Phil, we have all this on our doorstep and we don't even bother to explore more!'

The four-hour trip came to an end. 'Do you think we can claim this on expenses?' joked Abbey as they got off the boat.

'Don't know, but I doubt Richard would be happy to sign the cheque,' sniggered Phil.

They made their way into town and ventured into the President's Lodge terrace bar. This part of the hotel was open air, but the bar itself was protected by a thatched roof. It was packed with wooden tables and chairs and had a small circular pool in the middle, which was lit with underwater lights and looked very inviting to Abbey as she walked past it on her way to the bar. No, she quickly thought. Her swimming days at this hotel were firmly over.

The bar was already busy with tourists and punters finishing off their week with a well-earned drink. They took a small table by the stone wall overlooking the river.

'Cheers,' said Abbey, chinking her glass against Phil's.

Friday night was karaoke night, and the punters who had not spent the day drinking on the river safari were still reluctant to get up and sing. Phil motioned to the DJ to bring over the song sheets.

'Look Phil,' teased Abbey, 'if you sing Tom Jones again I'm away up that hill. Understand?'

Phil shouted his way through 'Mustang Sally' and Abbey quite happily provided the backing vocals in the chorus. The bar was soon packed with rangers and safari guides and the noise of laughter and voices got louder as the evening wore on. Most of the locals already knew Abbey and Phil from previous social occasions, and were happy to chat and buy them drinks.

Phil was also on the town football team and most of the rangers and guides were also players. Football was a favourite sport in Botswana and taken very seriously at any level. Each town or village usually had a football pitch or an area that was sacred and only used to play football on. Sundays were practice nights in Kasane, and it was not unusual for half the town to turn up and watch. On match days, the team could expect the whole town to come along and support them.

Not only did Phil enjoy football, but he had also mentioned to Abbey that his street cred had gone through the roof after he had been chosen to play for the first team, and he had become instantly attractive to the majority of the women in the town, regardless of their age!

After a couple more rounds of gin and tonics, they staggered back home. Abbey left Phil and made her way up the hill. She didn't notice Darren's bakkie parked outside. She stumbled up the steps, fell into the fly screen and landed on her backside on the lounge floor with a loud thud.

Darren turned and looked at her from the kitchen. 'So, this is what you get up to when I'm not around,' he said jokingly.

'I'll have you know,' slurred Abbey, waving her hand in the air, 'I've been on a team-building day, and now I love my colleagues, *very, very*, much.' With that, she curled up into a ball and went to sleep on the floor, exactly where she had landed.

She woke up in bed, completely naked. Her head felt like it was going to explode. Darren appeared at the bedroom door with two cups of coffee.

'How's the head this morning?'

'Shhh, not so loud,' whispered Abbey, trying to move off the pillow, fumbling in the bedside drawer for paracetamol tablets.

'Come on then, tell me all about your team-building day.'

Abbey sat up and told the story in as much detail as she could remember.

'Monday should be an interesting day then,' laughed Darren. 'Assuming that Richard has a sense of humour?'

'Well, if he has, it certainly hasn't seen the light of day for some time,' replied Abbey. 'I have never met such an incompetent arse in my life. Were you due back yesterday? I don't remember seeing your bakkie when I came home.'

'Yes, I told you I'd be back on Friday at some point, and to be quite honest I'm surprised you can remember anything about coming home!'

He smiled as he watched her trying to swallow whole paracetamol tablets with hot coffee, choking in the process.

'I feel like shit,' muttered Abbey, taking another slurp of her coffee and slumping back onto the pillow.

'And I have just the hangover cure you need,' said Darren, pulling back the duvet.

Chapter Nine

A warm breeze blew through the kitchen window. Richard was sitting at the kitchen table, feet up, his hands resting on the back of his head. He had showered and changed into clean clothes after the disastrous morning down by the river. His contempt for his colleagues had gone from simmering to boiling point. That was it - they had gone too far this time. He had no choice but to take action if he was to re-establish any kind of control over the two imbeciles he had been lumbered with. He picked up the phone and rang the Savuti Lodge.

Mr Permelo listened without a word.

'Ja,' he finally spoke. 'The girl is a problem now this Darren Scott has appeared on the scene. We should have sorted her out months ago.'

Richard sighed and agreed they might have missed their opportunity. 'Wait though,' he said. 'Mr Scott works away a lot. I'm sure it would be quite easy to find out when his next trip is.'

'Ja, that would be good,' snarled Mr Permelo. 'You let me know straight away.'

'What about the buffoon, Phil?' asked Richard. 'Any ideas about him?'

Mr Permelo laughed into the phone. 'Ah yes, Mr Phil. Now that is an easy one. I have a plan that will finish him off for good.'

Richard replaced the receiver, feeling much better. *This house was far too small*, he thought, as he looked around the kitchen. He thought it grossly unfair that Abbey Harris had been given the bungalow at the top of the hill - *the* bungalow he had been asking to live in for the past six months ever since Abbey's predecessor had left Kasane.

He took a deep drag from his cigarette and blew the bluish smoke in the direction of the open window. Although he knew that Abbey hadn't specifically requested the house, given that she didn't even know it existed until she arrived, it was typical of that sort of woman - bossy and in your face - to end up with the best of everything. His own house had only one bedroom and a small rectangular garden with no evidence of any living foliage. It was near the centre of town and the constant barking from the neighbourhood dogs nearly drove him demented. He had been in Kasane just over a year now and, apart from the house, it had been a very good decision.

Richard had started his teaching career at the age of twenty-six. He had taken the longer route of going to college before university, where he finally graduated (without honours), with a degree in Engineering, before completing his PGCE at Glasgow University. He had left school at sixteen and had been taken on as apprentice with a local builder. It soon dawned on Richard, and his employer, that getting his hands dirty and working out in sub zero temperatures in the middle of winter was not what Richard was cut out for.

After a brief spell of working in local shops, stacking shelves and being rude to customers, he was beginning to wonder what would bring contentment and the financial independence he craved. It was his mother who suggested he went to the local college to see what courses they had on offer. After initially rebuking the suggestion, Richard signed up to do a HND in construction, a qualification that would allow access onto a degree course.

Richard lived with his mother until he left for Glasgow University. His father had left the family home when he was five years old and, apart from an old family photograph he knew his mother still kept hidden in the bottom of a drawer in her bedroom, Richard had very little memory of him. He had been brought up in relative poverty, wearing second-hand clothes and existing on the most basic of diets. His mother had tried to work, but her back problems had prevented any further employment and, from the age of ten, Richard had been brought up on benefits and hand-me-downs from the locals in the village.

His school life had been hard because of it, with name-calling and bloody noses, as some of the bullies in the class never missed an opportunity to inflict some sort of physical injury. Finally, in 1977, Richard embarked on his first teaching job in a secondary school in Carlisle, about thirty miles from the village.

Richard found teaching a much more preferable form of employment than any job he had done so far. For the first time in his life he had power. Power over other people – the pupils. Richard soon learned that he could shout - actually, he could bellow - down a corridor and make the windows reverberate in their frames. He had missed out on the good old days when teachers were able to throw board rubbers and crack pupils' knuckles with a ruler, but he still had tried and trusted methods, most of which were carried out in the darkness and privacy of the store room, which could render the hardest of students to a gibbering wreck. Richard had been very content for over fifteen years and been promoted to head of department, when a new head teacher arrived at the school.

Mrs Ryan had been appointed after a damning Ofsted Inspection, which had labelled the school as 'failing'. She had stalked the corridors, carried out impromptu lesson observations and demanded to see evidence of lesson planning. Within six months, the staff turnover had doubled and Richard found himself working with two new colleagues. He had so far managed to keep his head down and away from the attention of the abominable Mrs Ryan, whom he had attempted to fob off on her first visit to the technical department with folders of paperwork and pupil projects. He knew it would not work a second time, and he was more than happy to let his new, younger colleagues set up teaching folders and schemes of work.

As well as the new paperwork regime, other procedures that simply went against the grain with Richard were also put in place. Department development plans and regular staff meetings were all now part of teaching life. Was there no stopping this control freak of a woman, who seemed to want to know about everything that shouldn't concern her?

The 'O' level and subsequent GCSE results of Richard's classes had always been below average, and it wasn't long before Mrs Ryan had demanded a meeting to discuss why the classes of his less experienced colleagues were outperforming his. It was at the end of this particularly harrowing meeting that Richard had gone off sick with his first bout of food poisoning, followed by stress. Eventually, he spent more time at home (being paid), than he did in school.

After his sixth month off sick, he received a letter from the Director of Education, stating he had been given early retirement on ill-health grounds. Richard had reluctantly accepted the incredibly insulting offer, even though it dramatically reduced his pension, but he knew going back to work for Mrs Ryan was not an option. He also knew that his methods and teaching styles were not looked upon favourably by the new powers that resided in the education offices at the local council. He banked his cheque as soon as possible.

Before leaving for Botswana, Richard had spent the last few years picking up supply work and claiming benefits. The position at AVP was too good to be true and Richard wasted no time in applying. His elderly mother had been moved into sheltered accommodation and he really couldn't see any reason not to break free. He had no real friends to speak of and, apart from one disastrous date with a fellow teacher from the English department, his love life was non-existent. He and women just didn't get on. They were a funny breed and Richard had resigned himself to the fact that romance would never be an option in his life. However, being a virgin in his forties was not something

Richard would ever share with anyone, although his mother probably knew as he had moved back in with her immediately after leaving Glasgow.

Two weeks later, after an interview in Manchester at the charity's head office, he had been given the news that his application was successful and he should be ready to leave the United Kingdom within three months. Kasane had turned out to be the best thing that had happened to Richard in a long time. He had met like-minded people like Mr Permelo, who had introduced possibilities into Richard's life that, in the past, he had only ever been able to dream about. That part of his life was a long way away now and, if Mr Permelo kept to his part of the bargain, it would never be a problem again.

A knock at the front door broke his train of thought. He looked at the clock. It was four o'clock on the dot. *Ah good*, he thought to himself, *another interview*. He quickly went into the bedroom and sprayed on the aftershave his mother had bought him as a leaving present, before opening the door.

Chapter Ten

The beginning of the working week arrived all too quickly for Abbey. Richard did not mention the team-building day, but instead bustled about the office as if nothing untoward had happened at all. Abbey looked at Phil quizzically who shook his head and smiled.

'Oh Richard, before I forget. I need to see the holiday booking forms,' shouted Abbey as Richard made his way out of the door.

Phil immediately looked up at Abbey, 'Where are we off to, then?'

'Darren's got to go to Cape Town for a meeting with some surveyors. He's asked me to go with him.'

'Fab.'

'Yeah, I've never been and I'm really looking forward to it. We're going to fly down tomorrow.'

Without any comment at all, Richard put the form on her desk. Abbey filled it out to request two weeks' holiday, to start from the next day.

'Going to manage without me, Phil?' she teased.

'Oh yeah, it's going be a laugh a minute with Captain Pugwash over there,' sighed Phil, motioning his hand at Richard, who was checking the compost bags outside.

'You're in a good mood this morning,' commented Abbey a little later, as Phil sang quietly to himself.

'Yep, that's because I have a hot date tonight.'

Abbey raised her eyebrows. 'Do I know the lucky girl?'

'Doubt it; she works in the office at one of the hotels. I hardly know her myself. She came around the house at the weekend, bold as brass, and asked me out.'

'Must be your football skills,' laughed Abbey.

'Or the fact that I am completely irresistible to all women!'

Very early the next morning, Abbey and Darren flew down to Gaborone Airport and then boarded a South African Airlines plane to Cape Town. They hired a car and Darren drove towards the town, Abbey instantly noticing and appreciating the cooler temperature.

'Where are we staying?' she asked, admiring the views around her, looking up in the direction of Table Mountain.

'I've booked us into a small hotel at Hout Bay,' replied Darren. 'It's not far out of town and the beach is great.'

'Wow!' gasped Abbey when they turned into the bay and onto the main promenade, which was lined with street cafés and restaurants. 'What are those trees called?' she asked, pointing to a line of tall trees, abundant with purple flowers.

'Those are Jacaranda trees. You can see them all over South Africa. They're beautiful, aren't they?'

The beach seemed to stretch for miles, and the views all around them were stunning with the most amazing houses positioned on the cliff, overlooking the bay. After checking in at the hotel, they spent the rest of the afternoon paddling and relaxing on the sand. The sun was hot but the breeze was exhilarating, and Abbey suddenly realised just how much she missed the sea. Not that Manchester was by the sea, but at least a beach was easily accessible, and you didn't have to drive through other countries for days just to get a paddle. Living in a land-locked country somehow seemed to make the heat even more inescapable.

After a couple of days relaxing and following the tourist trails, they went into Cape Town. Darren had a meeting at ten-thirty so Abbey, armed with her credit cards, hit the shopping boulevard by the water's edge. Now these were what she called clothes shops! Fashion in Kasane started and finished with the PEP store and Abbey had decided, on her first visit to PEP, she would probably rather walk round naked than wear any of the clothes available out of there. The Motswana people seemed to have a unique fashion style all of their own, and it was not unusual to see a pair of striped trousers, a checked jacket and a polka-dot shirt, all part of one ensemble, walking proudly down the street!

As she wandered around the boutiques, she started to feel quite underdressed as she noticed how smart most of the South African women looked and the care they obviously took about their appearance. She smiled, remembering her own morning routine before leaving for work back in Manchester. What would the then Abbey have thought of the now Abbey, in her cropped jeans and a cotton shirt, comfortably browsing around the shops?

By late afternoon, she had exhausted all the boutiques and was laden with shopping bags. She went to meet Darren outside at a café on the harbour.

'Get everything you need?' he smiled with a slight tone of sarcasm in his voice at the sight of the glossy plastic bags hanging off her arms.

'Yeah, I think so.'

'What about another suitcase to pack them all into?' he joked, embracing her warmly.

'Listen you, I've not had any retail therapy for months now, and I was getting serious withdrawal symptoms. Anyway, less about me - how did your meeting go?' she asked.

'OK, I think we're on track to deliver on time, although the suppliers are stoking up the pressure to get samples in sooner rather than later.'

Abbey wasn't entirely convinced he was as confident as he was trying to make out. After a quick cup of coffee, watching the boats sail in and out of the harbour, they headed back to the hotel.

'I've booked a table at the fish restaurant on the beach for seven-thirty,' said Darren when they had parked up.

'Oooh lovely,' replied Abbey. 'Now I can wear some of my new acquisitions.'

The fish restaurant was a wooden, two-storey building, which stood on the sand. The seating area was upstairs to make the most of the views across the water. Abbey and Darren had been given a table by the window.

'Umm, this food is just exquisite!' she mumbled, as she ate her way through a plate of fresh oysters, lobster and the hugest prawns she had ever seen.

Darren watched her and smiled. 'I knew you'd like it,' he said, pouring her another glass of wine.

They watched the sun set on the horizon. It shimmered and went into an oval shape before vanishing into the Atlantic Ocean.

'Come on, we'll finish off the evening with a walk on the beach,' said Darren, taking her hand.

'I'll have to take these heels off first,' she giggled.

There wasn't a cloud in the sky and the moon shone brightly casting streaks of silver light, which glistened and danced on top of the waves. Darren stopped on the wet sand just inches from the edge of the water, took hold of Abbey's shoulders and looked directly at her.

'Abbey,' he whispered, 'are you happy?'

'Of course I am. I can't remember ever being happier.'

Darren took a deep breath and exhaled slowly.

'What is it?' asked Abbey slightly concerned. 'Is there something wrong?'

'No, not wrong exactly.' His grip tightened on her shoulders. 'Abbey, I love you and I want to spend the rest of my life with you.'

Abbey's eyes widened as she took a sharp intake of breath at what she had just heard. 'Are you proposing?' she asked.

'Would you like me to?'

'Try it and see!'

Darren took both her hands in his and squeezed tightly. 'Abbey Harris, will you marry me?'

She dropped her shoes on to the sand and threw her arms around his neck. 'Of course I will. Oh my god, I can't believe it!' she squealed.

He wrapped his arms around her waist, lifted her up, and kissed her passionately as the water lapped around his feet.

Phil looked at himself in the mirror. He had showered and shaved, and even ironed his shirt. He ruffled his hair with his hands. He couldn't believe his luck. Ka Ka was one of the hottest girls in town. He had admired her from afar at the weekly football matches, trying to catch her eye, but always kept his distance given she was never short of male attention.

He went over the Sunday afternoon once again in his head. He had been lying in his hammock in the garden in the shade, quietly daydreaming. Her voice had woken him.

'I saw you from the road,' she smiled. 'I have watched you play football lots of times. Would you like some company?'

Ka Ka had stayed for the afternoon and Phil had enjoyed himself immensely. She chatted about her family and childhood days in Gaborone. She had come to Kasane after the promise of a good job in the hotel. In turn, he had described what it was like growing up in Sheffield, and his love of Sheffield United and football in general. She had smiled at him and nodded when he had asked her to go out for dinner with him the next evening.

Phil had booked a table at the President's Lodge. He was determined to make an effort to impress in the hope of having a stable relationship. He was happy living in Kasane and, although Richard was enough to send a saint over the edge, he enjoyed his work, and the friendship that he and Abbey shared helped to keep Richard's petulant manner in perspective. Abbey had got herself sorted and was now happily living with Darren, and he was keen to follow suit in finding a suitable partner.

Ka Ka arrived at seven o'clock prompt. She looked lovely and had obviously gone to a lot of trouble. She wore a long, deep red dress, which fell beautifully over her tall, slim figure. She had long pleated hair extensions, which fell effortlessly around her shoulders. Phil could barely believe he was taking her out on a date.

71

After a drink in the bar, they were shown to their table. Phil had requested a window seat so they could sit and eat their dinner whilst enjoying the evening breeze. Ka Ka seemed happy to listen to him and laugh at his jokes, although he wasn't quite sure whether either his Yorkshire accent or northern sense of humour had really been understood. The conversation and wine seemed to flow freely, and it wasn't long before Ka Ka felt comfortable enough to talk about her own likes and dislikes about the town.

As Phil paid the bill, he decided that the evening had been a complete success. 'Would you like me to walk you home?' he asked as they left the hotel.

'My house is past yours,' she laughed, 'so I will walk you home.'

They stopped outside the small bungalow. Ka Ka held out her hand and Phil took hold of it and kissed it, his lips touching her warm, soft skin.

'Would you like to come in for a beer or coffee?'

'Would you like me to?'

'Most definitely,' he replied, as he led her towards the front door.

Next morning, the sound of bird song in the trees outside the window gently woke Phil out of a deep slumber. He couldn't remember ever having such a good night's sleep, and outstretched his arm to the other side of the bed. He looked over, slightly surprised that Ka Ka had gone without waking him. He made his way to work, smiling happily and looking forward to the day ahead.

Richard was also in a good mood, which Phil put down to Abbey's absence. The time seemed to drag by with Phil continually looking at the clock. He spent most of the day working outside with a spade under the hot sun. This was also the first day in a long time that he hadn't felt hung over, and it felt good.

With the help of two school pupils who were on the volunteers list, he planted all the trees that had been waiting under the shading.

Richard had been acting quite strangely, coming and going from the office without a word about what he was doing.

Whilst digging holes in the hard earth, Phil had made up his mind to call in at the Savuti on his way home to see Ka Ka, and hopefully arrange another date. He was still glowing inside and hoped that she felt the same way and would be happy to go out with him again.

So, later that day, he walked into the cool hotel reception and waited patiently for the receptionist to come off the phone.

'Dumela Mma,' he said eventually when the woman still hadn't looked in his direction after replacing the receiver. 'Can you tell Ka Ka that Phil is here to see her?'

Still without acknowledging him, the receptionist called over to the door man and spoke in Setswana. He disappeared behind one of the office doors. Phil waited, tapping his fingers on the counter. The receptionist looked up and tutted at the noise. Phil put his hands in his pockets. After a couple of minutes, the doorman reappeared and spoke to the receptionist.

She looked at Phil. 'I am sorry, but Ka Ka has gone home already. Would you like to leave her a message?'

'No, it's fine. I'll catch up with her some other time.'

Phil left the hotel feeling slightly disappointed and turned left onto the road in the direction of Ka Ka's house. As he walked along the road, his stomach rumbled and he was aware of sweat running down his face. He didn't feel particularly hot and smiled to himself, wondering whether he was in fact going into detox from not having a serious drinking session for well over forty-eight hours.

Ka Ka wasn't at home, and the woman who opened the door seemed reluctant to give out any information. Eventually, after some gentle questioning, Phil learned that Ka Ka had been sent to Francistown to work in one of the hotels there to cover for someone who was off sick.

'How long will she be away, Mma?' asked Phil, now holding his stomach, which was getting extremely painful, cramps shooting from one side to the other.

The woman shrugged her shoulders and waved her hands in the air. 'How would I know these things?' she shouted angrily, before shutting the door.

Chapter Eleven

When Abbey returned to work after her holiday in Cape Town, Phil was nowhere to be seen. Abbey was desperate to tell him her news and was disappointed when he still hadn't arrived by nine o'clock.

'Richard, has Phil got the day off today?'

'Not as far as I am aware. Come to think of it, I've not seen him for over a week now.'

'What?' exclaimed Abbey, absolutely horrified at Richard's indifference. 'He might be ill. Did you not think to check?'

'Look Abbey, he's a big boy now. I think he can look after himself.'

There was a hint of malevolence in Richard's voice which made Abbey feel slightly uncomfortable. 'Well, I'm going to see if he's OK,' she said, leaving the office before Richard had the chance to object.

She walked as quickly as she could up the main street to the small bungalow. Phil had already taken time off work from what was known as 'sleeping sickness', which was transmitted by the dreaded tsetse fly that thrived in warm, damp, shady places such as those along the riverbanks of the Chobe. Fortunately, Kasane Clinic was well equipped to deal with this affliction, as well as malaria, caught from the mosquitoes, which also bred abundantly in the Chobe National Park and were an aggressive killer of adults and children.

When Abbey arrived at the bungalow, Phil was sitting on the steps outside the door, his head in his hands. Abbey walked up the garden path towards him.

'Phil,' she said, as she sat next him and put her hand on his shoulder. 'Phil, what's the matter? What's wrong?'

'I've fucked up big time, Abbey. I really have. I can't believe I could have been so stupid.' He looked up at her. His voice was weak and his face drained of any colour.

'Look, whatever it is can't be that bad. I'm sure it'll all work out and…'

'Abbey, I'm HIV.'

She looked at him in silence.

'Did you hear me? I'm HIV.'

Abbey took his shoulders and turned him to face her. Her eyes were welling up with tears and, without saying a word, she put her arms around his neck and hugged him as hard as she could. Phil broke down and held on to her as if he was holding on for dear life. Neither of them moved. It was Phil who spoke first.

'I'm gonna have to go home, hun. Got to get drugs and all that.'

'When did you find out?' whispered Abbey.

'A couple of days ago. I had to go to the clinic the beginning of last week. I kept being sick and my stomach felt as though it was tied up in knots. I'd eaten at the President's Lodge the night before and thought I'd probably got food poisoning. Instead of getting better it got worse, so I dragged myself along to the clinic. Anyway, they gave me rehydration salts and took all sorts of samples. They said it was just routine and they needed to do tests. I didn't think anything of it, because after a few days I felt as right as rain again.'

'Did you tell Richard you were ill?'

'Yeah, I sent a note with the kid next door. He never got in touch or asked me when I'd be back at work, so I milked it a bit and took the whole week off. I was going to go back, but then I got a letter through the door asking me to make an appointment with Doctor Mapuntsi immediately. She told me they had identified the bug that had made me ill, and then dropped the bombshell about the other test they'd done. She was really nice about it and explained to me what my options were. I've been thinking of nothing else for three days now.'

'Why the hell didn't you ring me?'

76

'Look, there was nothing you could do. Anyway, there was no chance I was going to spoil your holiday, especially given it's the first one you've had since you got here!'

'What would you like me to do? Can I help you in any way?' she asked, stroking the back of his head.

'Nah, I'm OK. Got a flight sorted for Friday of this week. Rang Head Office and told them my mother was really ill and I needed to go and visit her immediately. They didn't quibble at all and booked my ticket within the hour.'

'Hell, I'm going to miss you Phil,' she said, hugging him again.

'Listen, there *is* something you can do. Will you sort this out with Richard? I can't face him and I'm not going into the office again.'

'Oh course I will, leave him to me. Look, do you want to come and stay with me until Friday? I don't like leaving you here on your own.'

'What, and move into the lurve nest?' he smiled. 'How was Cape Town, anyway?'

'It was good - no, it was great, but let's just talk about you for now.'

They talked for about an hour, going over everything that needed to be done. Abbey was going to take Moxy, Phil's adopted cat, although she wasn't completely sure that Moxy would agree to moving into her bungalow and would probably run away.

Abbey left Phil packing some boxes and decided to go straight home rather than the office. Richard could wait. She sat outside on the veranda, watching the busy weaverbirds continue with their own daily routine, yet barely noticing them, when Darren's bakkie drove up the driveway.

'Hey, you OK?' he shouted. 'I've just bumped into Richard in town. He said you had gone off somewhere and not come back.'

She stood up as he approached her. 'Come here, please,' she said in a quiet voice, holding out her hands.

Darren walked over to her and took her into his arms. Unable to control herself any further, she promptly burst into tears. She had wanted to cry since Phil had first told her about his condition, but felt somehow it wouldn't have been fair on him.

'Don't let me go, not just yet.'

'I have no intention of doing so,' he whispered in her ear.

Darren persuaded Abbey to take the rest of the day off and said he would call into the office and sort things out with Richard. That was a huge relief to Abbey, who wasn't sure how she was going to tell him or how she might deal with his reaction, especially if it lacked the same compassion it had after the road accident. She decided she would also take the next couple of days off and spend them with Phil before he left Kasane. Darren was also going to be the bearer of this news to Richard. She knew that Richard would not argue with Darren in any way and there would be no problems when she went back to work.

After Abbey had left, Phil sat on the lounge floor surrounded by cardboard boxes. He looked around at the bare walls with an overwhelming desire to try and make sense of the situation, of his life so far. His time in Kasane had been the happiest he could remember, and he wondered if there was any possibility of holding onto it a bit longer. He abandoned the box packing and walked down the main street through the town. Without thinking, he veered to the left and went into Banjo's and sat on his usual stool at the bar.

He remembered his first visit here over eight months ago. He had been on his way to see Abbey to compare houses, when the loud music and sounds of laughter had drawn his attention and fuelled his curiosity. The bar was a small, rectangular room with a pool table by the window and a jukebox on the wall. Apart from a few chairs and tables scattered about the concrete floor, there was nothing else in the room. The smell of stale smoke and body odour hit his nostrils as soon as he walked through the door. The barman on duty had served Phil on his first visit without uttering one word, just a nod of the head as money was exchanged. Within five minutes of being in the bar, he had felt a hand touch his arm, and a voice whispering down his ear.

'Me nice,' said the soft voice. 'Me nice and only fifty pula for you nice guy.'

The attention from the women, who seemed to adore him, had made him feel special again. They hung on to his every word and he felt flattered, a feeling he hadn't felt since the first weeks of courtship with Debra. His visits to the bar had got more regular and he had desperately tried to resist the temptation, but always managed to find a reason to go, which would outweigh any reason to stay away.

Phil snapped his mind back to his current situation. He looked around the room. The same faces, the same conversations, the same scene playing itself out, over and over, in every seedy, backstreet brothel across the globe. No matter what avenue his thoughts took him, he always came to the same conclusion. He had no one but himself to blame. He had lived through the last eight months making conscious decisions that he knew could jeopardise his health and his future.

He pushed away his beer and made his way to the door, keeping his eyes focused directly in front, until he stepped out into the bright sunshine. He wondered what Debra would say to him now.

Debra had grown up on the next street to Phil in his home town of Sheffield, and they had been together since year eleven at secondary school. They had not got married, but Phil had moved into her parents' house whilst they saved up for a deposit for their own flat. When Debra fell pregnant, Phil had promised to turn his life around and start providing for the three of them. In a bid to prove to her, and to himself, that he was not the 'useless piece of shit' she constantly called him, he had enrolled on a teaching degree course at Manchester Metropolitan University. He secured a room in the nearby town and managed to get through the first six weeks with relative ease, even submitting his first assignment on time.

Phil's first teaching practice had been arranged at one of the secondary schools not far from the university campus. The school was a large comprehensive, situated on the foot of a council estate. It did not have a good academic record, and a recent Ofsted inspection had highlighted weaknesses in several areas. Phil knew it was not going to be an easy first ride but, having come from a similar background himself, it gave him some reassurance he would cope. The first couple of days had been merely observation of the other teachers in the department, and to give him time to organise his lesson plans.

His first day of teaching finally arrived and the period one lesson was the year ten computing class. Phil had sat in this class before and was confident that he had planned a good lesson, which would keep them busy for the whole hour. He arrived at the classroom in plenty of time, clutching his prepared worksheets, still warm from the photocopier.

He smiled confidently as the pupils noisily took their seats and waited for complete silence before starting the lesson. He had not even finished his introduction when a dark-haired, slim boy with a face full of freckles, sitting on the front row, interrupted him. Phil thought he had answered the question adequately, but the boy, dissatisfied with the response, challenged his every statement, taking delight in ridiculing the new student teacher with his own extensive knowledge of the Internet. Phil's initial tactic had been to humour the boy, and laugh along with the class as they laughed at him. Within fifteen minutes, his careful planning had been destroyed and the lesson quickly turned into an annihilation of Phil's character and ability as a teacher.

His initial disappointment at their reluctance to learn quickly turned into frustration. He walked over to the boy who had started the mêlée and said in a voice loud enough to be heard at the back of the room, 'Do you *think* you could stay quiet long enough for me to finish a sentence?'

The boy sneered and stole a glance backwards at his peers, savouring his moment of triumph in succeeding to disrupt the class.

'I asked you a question,' repeated Phil, his voice slightly more raised.

The boy fiddled with his ruler, tapping it on the desk and, without looking up, replied, 'If you said anything worth listening to, I might *think* about it.'

The class roared with laughter. The boy stood up, turned around, and took a low bow to his appreciative audience. Phil left the classroom and the school five minutes later, after locking the boy in the store cupboard and throwing the key out of the open window onto the flowerbed below. Debra had had a lot to say on that occasion when the letter dropped onto the mat, advising him that, 'due to unfortunate circumstances', he was no longer a student teacher at Manchester Metropolitan University.

Phil kicked at the dust as he walked back towards his bungalow. He still wondered what words Debra would use to describe his latest failure, although in his head he heard her quite clearly voicing her disgust and disappointment in him yet again. After the humiliation of the teaching practice, Phil had decided that the job with AVP would provide him with an opportunity to put some space between him and his problems. He had needed time to think. The baby was due at any time, his head was close to bursting point, and the looks of disappointment from Debra's parents were grinding him down further. Recognising the first signs of depression, as he found it harder to get out of bed each morning, he decided to take the selfish route of self-preservation, and distance himself from all that he knew. He left the United Kingdom that October morning under a cloud of misery and despair.

As he walked up the garden path, Moxy, the tabby cat he had taken in as an abandoned kitten, greeted him with a meow and rubbed herself around his ankles, making a low purring noise. The sight of unfinished packing greeted him as he walked inside. He had no doubt in his mind whatsoever the words Abbey would use if she turned up tomorrow, and had to finishing the packing boxes.

He deliberated whether or not to tell Abbey about Ka Ka. He had not seen her since their dinner date and he was now worried that she, too, would be infected and he had more or less sentenced her to death. Their too brief union had hurt him deeply and, although disappointed that he might never see her again, the thought of living with her death on his conscience was too much to bear.

He sat on the floor between the boxes, Moxy purring on his lap, tears falling onto her soft fur.

Abbey spent the following day helping Phil to clear out his house. She had borrowed the bakkie from AVP, loading it up with mops, brushes and disinfectant.

'Honestly Phil,' exclaimed Abbey, cleaning a second kitchen cupboard. 'Have you ever cleaned in here, ever?'

Eventually, all the possessions that Phil wanted to take home were boxed and labelled. Abbey had arranged for them to be picked up by the freight company she had used to bring her own items over from the UK. They put a sign on the gate saying 'house sale' and any unwanted items disappeared within the hour without a single tebe changing hands.

Darren sent two of his labourers to tidy the garden and, at sunset, as the garden gate whined closed for the last time, the bungalow looked well-kept and cared for. Abbey told Phil she had made up the spare room and that he would spend his last night at her house and sleep in a clean bed. She would not take no for an answer and Phil made very little objection.

Phil left Kasane on the Friday morning. After an emotional farewell, Abbey drove the short distance from the small airport back to the office in silence, preferring not to put the CD player on. Richard was out at the primary school when she got back, which gave her peace and quiet to think as she looked at Phil's empty chair.

She had known about his lifestyle and the time he had spent in the local bars, which were full of men and women touting their bodies for money. They had never spoken about this part of African life, and Phil had preferred that this part of his life should remain confidential. Abbey was more than happy about this, as she did not want to judge Phil and ruin the close friendship that had developed.

Abbey left the office just after two. The heat was exhausting and she needed a break. She walked along to the junior school and around the back of the building to where the teachers' houses stood. The students were still in study classes and the whole campus was quiet. She knocked on Judith's door.

'Hi Abbey, come in. Mind the mess, won't you?'

The floor was covered in the familiar site of half-packed boxes and cases.

'Going somewhere?' asked Abbey, sitting on the arm of the chair.

Judith looked at her, sensing her mood. 'Are you alright? I heard that Phil left today. Abbey, I'm so sorry. I know how close you two were.'

Abbey nodded, trying desperately not to let the tears start again.

'Is he going to be alright?' asked Judith, suggesting to Abbey that Phil's condition was already common knowledge. She wondered whether they had Richard to thank for that, who wouldn't have missed any opportunity to convey the news to anyone who would listen. Not that being HIV positive in Botswana was unique, but people still valued their privacy and preferred to detach themselves away from their condition by getting on with daily life.

'Yes, I'm sure he's going to be fine. He's promised to keep in touch and, with modern technology and science, he stands a damn good chance.'

She pointed to the boxes and looked at Judith.

'Oh yes. My contract's up this week, dear.'

'Do you not want to stay on? Did they offer to renew it?'

'Well, yes they did, but it's this heat you know. And you have to admit, there's not much to do here.'

Abbey suddenly wondered when Judith had turned into such a party animal that the social life in Kasane had become inadequate.

'When do you leave?'

'I'm booked on the Monday flight.'

'Looks as though I'm going to lose two friends in one week then,' sighed Abbey. 'Would you like to come round tomorrow evening, for a farewell meal?'

Judith nodded. 'That would be lovely, dear.'

As she walked home, Abbey realised that friendships in ex-pat communities tended to be short-lived as people moved on regularly, and was something she would have to get used to the longer she stayed. She comforted herself knowing that, if and when Darren ever left Kasane, she would be by his side.

Chapter Twelve

Phil stepped out into the warm, spring air at Heathrow Airport. He hadn't slept and couldn't even remember which films had been playing throughout the journey. He fumbled his way through customs and security, still not grasping the reality of the situation. A hand on his shoulder made him stop and turn.

'Would you come this way please, sir?' A customs officer beckoned him towards a small office. 'Have you anything to declare sir?' asked the man, who Phil reckoned could only be in his early twenties.

'No.'

'Are you sure, sir? Because we have the power to search your belongings.'

Phil put both his case and hand luggage on the desk. 'It's not locked,' he said, looking at the young customs officer.

The young man unzipped the case and took each item out. Phil smiled as he remembered the argument he had had with Abbey before he had left.

'Look Phil, these clothes stink. They have to be washed; you just never know who might see them.'

He had looked at Darren for support, who had suggested that he should just humour Abbey. They had sat out on the veranda drinking cold beers, whilst Abbey busily sorted out clothes into different piles on the kitchen floor.

He could hear in his head the comments she would make if she ever found out about his bags being searched. Abbey had no qualms about ever saying, 'See I told you so' to anyone. He was sure he had seen Richard turn a pale green on several occasions when Abbey's predictions had come true.

'Thank you, sir. You are free to carry on with your journey.'

Phil picked up his luggage and headed for the train connection which would take him directly to Sheffield.

His parents, who were not expecting him back, looked at one another as he threw his bags onto the hall floor but, much to his relief, did not ask him any questions.

Exactly one week later, Phil was sat in the waiting room at the GP surgery. He looked around at the other people waiting to be seen. Some had coughs and colds, whilst others had absolutely nothing visibly wrong with them at all.

Just like me, he thought to himself. *Would they all stare at me if they knew? Would they sit next to me?* He wondered what it would be like having to wear a badge saying 'Warning – HIV positive!'

He thought of the Jews being forced by the Nazis to wear the Star of David, a sign to others that they were the cursed race. Was he part of a cursed race now? He still hadn't told his parents why he had come back home, and they hadn't asked. He knew he would have to eventually. But how to tell them he was terminally ill, and probably responsible for the illnesses and subsequent deaths of god knows how many others, at that moment, was beyond his emotional capability.

'Mr Phillip Brown to room seven,' said the receptionist, without looking up from her computer screen.

Phil walked into the office and closed the door behind him.

Chapter Thirteen

After Phil's departure, life in Kasane was not the same for Abbey. She felt she now had no other social outlets apart from Darren and barely left his side when he was home. Darren didn't mind the extra attention and supported Abbey as much as he could by showering her with affection. Abbey's life started to revolve around Darren's work and social commitments, and she would always join him on any weekend excursions. She was keen to bring the marriage date forward and suggested they got married on the next trip to Francistown. Darren agreed, and they married in a small registry office, exactly one month after Phil had left. They had two witnesses, a waiter from the hotel and the secretary at the registry office. They did not buy wedding outfits, instead choosing to wear plain, casual clothes.

They told nobody about their plans beforehand and returned immediately to Kasane, Abbey wearing the plain gold wedding band Darren had bought from the jewellers on the day of the wedding. Although the whole incident bore no hint of a celebration of two people declaring their undying love for one another, in Abbey's mind there was absolutely no question that she had done the right thing by getting married to Darren, and couldn't imagine life without him.

Abbey could not muster the same enthusiasm for her work as she had done previously. Richard, as expected, had not attempted to discuss Phil's departure with Abbey at all. Principally, she thought, because he didn't have the communication skills to talk about anything on an emotional level, and also because he knew that Abbey would be fiercely defensive in protecting Phil's reputation.

AVP had not replaced Phil, and Abbey and Richard had taken on his tasks and divided them equally. Abbey had argued to keep the weekly drive down to the Crossroads to pick up the new trees.

'Do you think that's a good idea?' probed Richard. 'There is a lot of lifting to be done and it would take you much longer on your own.'

'Simple,' retorted Abbey. 'There are plenty of people in this town who would bend over backwards for the chance to earn a bit of extra money. Why don't we employ someone part-time, maybe three days a week, to help with the lifting and carrying that Phil used to do?'

'I'd have to check it with Head Office first.'

'Well, do that. It makes much more financial sense than sending someone else over from the UK.'

Richard looked at Abbey. It was the first time she had ever sounded so officious, and for a moment he got a glimpse of 'Abbey the Marketing Director'. Her efficient tone worked and Head Office agreed to the request, although Abbey had a sneaking suspicion on reading the e-mail that Richard had put it over as his idea!

After placing an advert on the notice board in the Spar, they received about fifty letters of application as well as a constant stream of people knocking on the door. Richard had made it quite clear that recruitment was his remit and Abbey was more than happy to just let him get on with it.

She returned from the Crossroads the next Wednesday lunchtime, absolutely exhausted. Isaac had helped her load the trees and had listened to Abbey vent her feelings on Phil's sudden departure and life in general without him. Isaac had also been fond of Phil and empathised with her rather than sympathised, which she felt Darren did, not that she thought he did it intentionally; he was just doing the best he could in very difficult circumstances.

She was reversing the bakkie into the AVP plot when Richard appeared at the office door with a young lady, who looked about nineteen years old.

'Ah Abbey, that is good timing,' he said leading the young lady by the arm towards her. 'This is Boitachello and she is going to be working with us on Tuesday, Wednesday and Thursday.'

'Oh, right,' said Abbey slightly confused at Richard's choice. 'Welcome.'

'OK, we'll see you tomorrow then Boitachello, eight o'clock sharp.'

The girl smiled nervously at Richard and left.

'Now, correct me if I'm wrong, Richard,' said Abbey wiping the sweat off her forehead, 'but weren't we supposed to be hiring a male to do the lifting and carrying we talked about? Remember that conversation? About a week ago now?'

'Well Abbey!' exclaimed Richard. 'You do surprise me. I would have thought you'd be the last one to ignore the Sex Discrimination Act.'

'Does it exist here?' she replied, totally taken aback with his remark.

'Oh, while I remember this came for you in the post this morning.'

Abbey took the white envelope from him. It was addressed to Miss Abbey Harris and she knew immediately it was from the printing company she worked for in Manchester. She walked back into the cool of the office and sat down before opening it.

The letter was short and to the point.

Dear Abbey

Your career break is officially due to finish in six weeks time. Please could you confirm in writing by e-mail/fax the date that you will be returning to work. In the meantime we hope that you are well and look forward to seeing you on your return.

Yours sincerely

Mr Colin Trump

Managing Director

Abbey closed her eyes and sighed. This is all she needed. She had known in the back of her mind that the date for her return was coming up, but had been too distracted with Phil and the wedding to pay much attention it. Darren would be away until Friday afternoon. She put the letter in her bag and decided it could wait until then.

Abbey waited until they had finished dinner that Friday evening, before handing the Darren the letter.

'Well, what are you going to do?' he asked.

'What can I do? Is your contract likely to finish in the next six weeks?'

'No, and I wanted to talk to you about that.' His voice sounded serious. 'It looks as though it's actually going to be extended for another four months. We're having problems on some of the sites and it's taking longer than we expected to get the samples we need.'

Abbey raised her eyebrows at him. 'What do you suggest I do then?' she implored.

'Well, why not ask AVP if they would be willing to extend your contract here for another six months, and ask your firm to release you until then?'

'Absolutely no go, not with Paradise Printing. It's company policy that you get a maximum of twelve months career break, and I had to really exert pressure on them for that.'

'What about AVP?' pushed Darren. 'I bet they would extend your contract.'

'Yeah, I think they would, but that would mean resigning from Paradise Printing.'

'Your decision, Abbey. It's up to you.'

'Not really,' muttered Abbey. 'I have absolutely no intention of leaving you here on your own for four months and just seeing you for a couple of weeks over Christmas. Nah, no way. I'll e-mail them on Monday and resign.'

She snuggled up to Darren on the sofa and watched TV, resting her head on his shoulder. To her, it was a question of importance and this man was now the most important aspect in her life.

Her mind drifted to her relationship with her father, who had always been present during her childhood, but she could count on one hand the number of meaningful conversations they had actually had. It had hurt her as a teenager, witnessing her friends' fathers queuing up to be the taxi driver to fetch and carry their little girls while hers was always conspicuous by his absence. Her father never resisted her mother's wishes, and if that meant disagreeing with Abbey, no matter the reason, he duly complied.

Abbey couldn't remember her parents picking up the phone and asking her how she was, either at home or in Botswana. It was always her who made the effort to call, making sure she didn't forget birthdays and anniversaries. Not that they ever forgot her birthday, but the 'from Mother and Father', handwritten inside the card, didn't seem to convey any sincerity at all.

She compared this to the bond Darren seemed to have with his family, who not only rang on a regular basis, but also insisted on talking to Abbey on the phone and introducing themselves to the newest member of the family. Darren often spoke about his father who had died of lung cancer a few years before. He had been an archaeologist, and had taken Darren away on trips during the school holidays. Reading between the lines, she could tell they had had a close relationship and Darren's father had passed his enthusiasm for nature and the planet onto his son.

'He must have been very proud of you when you graduated,' she had commented.

Darren smiled at her. 'Yeah, it was a good day. My mother's got photographs somewhere. I'll ask her to find them and send them over.'

Darren had asked Abbey about her parents, but she always managed to change the subject early into the conversation. She didn't really know how to explain to him the wall of silence between them, or their lack of interest in her life. After she had told them about her decision to take a career break to work for AVP, they had voiced they concern and disapproval, calling her naïve and reckless. After that, the subject of her 'little adventure', as her mother had referred to it, was never mentioned again. Darren sensitively stopped pursuing this line of questioning, knowing full well that all would be revealed at some point in the future.

Abbey also compared her parents' marriage with her own and was confident it would never go the same way. Her parents had slept in separate bedrooms since Abbey was thirteen years old, and seemed to exist in a pre-determined routine which involved shopping, eating and household chores. She could not remember them showing any affection towards each other, or her for that matter. Physical contact of any sort had been non-existent and something both her parents still avoided.

Her life with Darren included laughter, spontaneity and, most importantly, a genuine love for one another. Darren was her rock, her confidant, and her lover. He provided the stability in her life that nobody else had been able to offer. In fact, if she was honest with herself, she knew that his life had completely consumed hers.

Chapter Fourteen

Abbey sent the e-mails to Paradise Printing and then to AVP as soon as she got into work on Monday morning. The reply from AVP came back before lunch, offering Abbey a new contract until the end of May the following year. She was sure she had made the right, if not the only, decision open to her, but felt slightly apprehensive about leaving her secure and well-paid job, which had provided her with a comfortable standard of living for a number of years.

Putting that out of her mind, she busied herself with the paperwork that had piled up in her in-tray. There were over one hundred trees to be planted this week and she needed to organise with the secondary school to obtain at least twenty volunteers to help with the task. Getting the students from the school to volunteer wasn't a difficult job. The work was always carried out in the late afternoon, and the volunteers were allowed to go home after lunch the following day as a reward.

Abbey looked at the stock sheets. According to her, there should be at least fifty-five trees in their compost bags outside under the shading, waiting to be planted. She paused for a moment, and then got up to do a manual stock take. After three counts and forty-five trees later, Abbey gave up. She checked the stock sheets again to see if she had made a mistake. She hadn't and she made a mental note to mention it to Richard when he came in. Richard had been behaving even more strangely than usual, making excuses to go home early and come in late. However, Abbey had no interest whatsoever in Richard's out of office activities, and was always glad to have the office to herself.

Richard queried Abbey's concern about the missing trees when he returned, and carried out yet another manual stock.

'Maybe they've been stolen?' Abbey suggested.

'Maybe you picked up the wrong number last week at the Crossroads? I told you it was a big job to do on your own.'

'Hey, don't put this one on me, Richard. I made no mistake and, believe it or not, I can actually estimate the number of trees on any delivery quite accurately, without counting them. And I know how many saplings I need to order without having to rely on a computerised just-in-time stock system!'

Seething at his immediate doubt in her abilities, she rang the supplier and changed the number for the new delivery for the coming week.

Wednesday morning arrived and Boitachello was waiting at the gate promptly at eight o'clock.

'Morning Boitachello,' said Abbey. 'How are you today?'

'Fine Mma, how are you?'

'Fine,' replied Abbey, smiling at the usual civilities that had to be gone through in Botswana, before any business could ever be conducted. Not that she thought badly of it; on the contrary, she imagined people would get along much better if they adopted the same manners at home.

'You're coming with me this morning,' said Abbey, picking up the keys for the bakkie and motioning to Boitachello to climb aboard.

They drove in silence, listening to the music playing in the CD player. Abbey sang along happily as the wind teased through her hair.

'Are you enjoying your work?' asked Abbey eventually. Boitachello smiled and nodded. 'What did Richard, sorry Mr Morrison, ask you when you applied?' quizzed Abbey, wondering what interview criteria Richard had used in his selection process.

'He didn't ask me any questions,' replied Boitachello.

Abbey shot a look over the cab. 'Oh. How did you get the job then?'

'My mother knows Mr Morrison,' explained Boitachello nervously. 'She is his maid, and he is very good to us - I mean her.'

Ho, ho, ho, wait til Phil hears about this one! thought Abbey smiling, already hearing Phil's sarcastic comments in her head.

Whatever reservations Abbey had had about Boitachello's ability to do the job soon disappeared, as she proved herself to be a hard, reliable worker. They had the bakkie loaded in no time and, although Abbey was not enthusiastic to stay and eat brunch at the café as she had done in the days with Phil for company, they did however stay for a quick coffee before heading back to the office. They arrived back at Kasane a good forty-five minutes earlier than usual. As Abbey drove down the main street, she noticed a bakkie driving towards her, half filled with tree saplings.

'Who was driving that bakkie, Boitachello?' asked Abbey, pulling over. 'Do you know?'

'I think it was Mr Permelo,' replied Boitachello, 'from the Savuti Lodge'.

Mr Permelo's underhand ways in managing the hotel was common knowledge in town. He was also known for his temper, and part of the fixtures and fittings in his office included a sjambok. Sjamboks were widely used in Botswana and were a combination of a large whip and a stick. She had seen the shopkeepers chase the children with them if they got to close to the stock outside the shop, or begged too often from the tourists. Mr Permelo's stood permanently by his desk and, according to the hotel employees, it was used on a regular basis. Phil had also told her that he was an avid gambler, and that he had stabbed a man in the chest, just missing his heart, after losing one thousand pula in a poker game.

Abbey quickly did a U-turn in the middle of the road and followed the bakkie. It pulled left into the Savuti Safari Lodge and drove around the back of the hotel, to the kitchen entrance. Abbey jumped out of the truck as soon as it stopped and walked over to Mr Permelo, who was giving orders to the garden boys.

'Mr Permelo,' she said, 'could I have a quick word with you please?'

'Ja,' he replied. 'It's Abbey, isn't it? Abbey Harris from AVP?'

95

'Actually, it's Abbey Scott. Darren Scott's wife. And yes, I do work for AVP.'

The tactic worked and Mr Permelo shifted uncomfortably from one foot to another.

'Can I ask you where you got those tree saplings, please?'

'Ja, of course. I bought them from Mr Morrison. I think he is your boss!'

'Wrong again, Mr Permelo,' she shot back at him. 'There is nothing in my contract of employment that states that Mr Morrison is my boss. Let's just say I humour him! Now, how many trees do you have there?' said Abbey, pointing to the trees being unloaded by the garden boys.

'I told you Miss... er, Mrs Scott... I bought them just now. Do you want to see my receipt?'

'No need,' snapped Abbey. 'We don't sell tree saplings to anyone around here. They are the property of AVP and destined only for the official plantation sites.'

'But I have a receipt here, I will show you.'

'Mr Permelo, I don't care if you have a letter from the Queen of England. Those saplings are not for sale. Please load them into my truck and I will return them back to where they should be.'

Mr Permelo stared at Abbey for a couple of seconds and then shouted more orders impatiently at the garden boys to reload the saplings onto the AVP truck, before storming back into the hotel. As Abbey drove out of the hotel driveway, she noticed dozens of new trees planted around the hotel gardens. She drove back to the office determined to have this out with Richard and force the truth out of him.

Richard was sitting at his desk, feet up as per usual reading the local newsletter. Abbey marched into the office and threw the keys down onto the desk.

Richard looked up. 'You're back earlier than usual,' he commented, startled by her abrupt manner.

Abbey stared at him momentarily and then launched her attack.

'I have just recovered thirty trees from the Savuti Lodge Hotel which, Mr Permelo tells me, he has bought from you!' She stood in front of him, resting both her hands on his desk. 'Thirty trees which, when identified as missing stock, will no doubt once again be put down to my inability to count!'

'Abbey I can explain, there is certainly nothing untoward going on here!'

'Save it for Head Office, Richard. You either resign or I'll blow the whistle. It's up to you.'

Richard stood up, glaring at her.

'You've been waiting for any opportunity to get me out,' he spat at Abbey, as he picked up his jacket from the back of his chair and began to walk away. 'Ever since you lost your little friend, who obviously couldn't keep his dick in his pants.'

'Oh, and Richard,' called Abbey as he left, determined not to take the bait. 'Could you leave me the list of interview questions you used to select our newest recruit? Just in case I need to employ a new labourer.'

Richard resigned from AVP with immediate effect. Abbey assured Head Office that she would assume full responsibility and had everything under control. The regional manager took the news well and was more than happy with Abbey's capabilities. He assured her he would be in touch when the details of a replacement became available.

Abbey did not sack Boitachello, who had been standing nervously outside the office, but offered her a full-time position.

'As for your mother, Boitachello,' said Abbey, 'tell her to come to my house on Saturday morning at nine. I am in need of a house keeper, and I have a feeling that your mother will be in need of a job.'

Abbey returned home that evening feeling a touch of nostalgia. She had finally displayed the people skills, which had been instrumental in her rise to Marketing Director at Paradise Printing. Darren arrived home shortly after her, holding a bottle of wine.

'Who's been ruffling a few feathers today, then?' he grinned, pulling her close.

Abbey raised her eyebrows and laughed. 'Good god, can nothing happen in this town without the bush drums relaying the news across the National Park within minutes?'

'Actually, I bumped into Mr Kobe, the assistant manager at the Savuti Lodge, in town. He told me about your run-in with Mr Permelo.'

'Umm,' replied Abbey. 'Don't think he's too impressed with me. I hope there'll be no repercussions. This isn't the first time we haven't exactly seen eye to eye.'

'Don't worry about him, Abbey,' replied Darren, 'there are plenty of people in this town who have been crossed by him and would welcome the opportunity to see him either go to prison, or disappear. I think he'll keep his distance if he wants his antics to remain out of the hands of the police. Oh, and I don't mean PC Plod down the road either. The fraud squad in Francistown have been watching him for some time now. Believe me, his days in Kasane are coming to an end.'

'Do you know him quite well?'

'No, not really,' replied Darren. 'Let's just say I don't see eye to eye with him either.'

'Good God, this just gets worse!' she sighed. 'You know, about three months ago Phil told me that Mr Permelo stabbed someone at a poker game? Did you hear about that? Do you think it's true?'

Darren looked surprised at her question. 'Well, given Phil was at that poker game, I would say so!' he replied.

Later that night, Abbey was awoken by someone hammering on the front door. Darren was already out of bed. She listened to the voices, unable to make out what they were saying. She heard the door close and Darren came back into the bedroom.

'There's a fire at the AVP office. I said we'd be there as soon as possible.'

Without a second thought, Abbey was out of bed and pulling her jeans on. They arrived at the office within minutes. People were shouting and running around throwing buckets of water onto the flames. The trees under the netting were alight and the flames were licking the window frames of the office. Not far from the gate was a standpipe. Between them, Abbey and Darren managed to organise people into two lines, passing buckets back and to. The heat was intense and sparks were flying up into the air. Abbey prayed that they wouldn't take hold in the bush, as it hadn't rained properly for some weeks.

Bucket after bucket of water was thrown onto the fire. The local rangers arrived with blankets and stamped out any sparks which were burning away from the main fire. It was nearly dawn when the last flame was quenched.

Abbey thanked the villagers and rangers for their help. The whole drama had lasted about five hours and the first shafts of dawn light were breaking into the dark sky as she walked around, assessing the damage.

'We've lost all our new stock,' she sighed to herself, as she kicked the hot ashes with her foot. 'Every single bloody tree.'

Darren returned from the higher plantations, walking down the hill with two of the rangers. 'The second and third plantations are fine. Nothing's been touched there. How many trees do you reckon have been lost?'

Abbey did a quick calculation out loud. 'Well, I picked one hundred trees today from the Crossroads, and then there were the trees I recovered from the Savuti.' As she spoke the last sentence she looked at Darren.

He nodded, reading her thoughts. 'Seems to me that if Mr Permelo couldn't have those trees, nobody could.'

'It could have been Richard?' suggested Abbey.

'It could have been both of them,' replied Darren. 'Those two have been as thick as thieves for some time now. I wouldn't put anything past either of them.'

99

'You know, this job is hard enough with the elephants eating and destroying the trees, without the vindictive actions of an imbecile like Richard.' She paused, surveying the damage one more time. 'I'll have to ring head office tomorrow. Maybe they'll give me enough money this month to replace these ones. I hope they're insured?'

Darren scowled. 'They bloody well should be, although if foul play is involved I'm not sure if they'll be covered. Come on,' he said, taking Abbey's arm, 'there's nothing more that can be done here. Not for now, anyway.'

Chapter Fifteen

At nine o'clock precisely, a tall, slim lady dressed in a brightly-coloured frock and a straw hat walked up the drive and knocked on the door.

'Hi,' said Abbey. 'You must be Prisca, I've been expecting you.'

Prisca was Boitachello's mother, and previously Richard's maid. Abbey invited Prisca to sit down and offered her a cup of bush tea.

'Well Mma,' continued Abbey as they sat opposite one another in the lounge, 'I am going to be spending more time at the office now Mr Morrison has left, and I am looking for someone to come in and clean for me, just on week days. Would you be interested in working for me?'

Prisca smiled and nodded. 'Yes Mma, I would be very happy to come and work for you. I will start on Monday, if that is alright?'

'That's fine. Now tell me, what was Mr Morrison paying you?'

Prisca shifted in her chair uncomfortably before replying. 'He paid me one hundred and fifty pula a week.'

'OK, well I am going to pay you two hundred pula and you can start at eight and finish at three. Does that suit you?'

Prisca nodded her head, looking quite satisfied with the outcome of the meeting.

'How long did you work for Mr Morrison?' enquired Abbey.

'I went to work for him when I left the Savuti Lodge.'

'Oh,' said Abbey, 'I didn't know you'd worked there first.'

'Yes, but Mr Permelo said he'd have to let me go. Said there wasn't enough work for me to do, but that he knew someone who needed a maid straight away and he would give me a good reference. Mr Morrison hired me the day after.'

Abbey nodded her head as more of Richard's manipulative behaviour was being exposed. She decided against sharing her thoughts with Prisca, but would talk it over later with Darren.

Abbey made another cup of tea and the two women sat and chatted quite easily as Abbey learned snippets about Prisca's life. It never ceased to amaze Abbey how the people in this country survived the most unthinkable hardships, and yet emerged with pride and dignity, ready to face whatever life brought to their door next.

Prisca was originally from Shakawe on the west side of Botswana, close to the Namibian border. There had been no school for her to go to when she was a child, and she spent most of her childhood by her mother's side, learning how to cook, sew and till the land. The minister from the local church had taught her how to read and write Setswana, on a Sunday, after the service - a skill that her father considered completely unnecessary for a young woman. He had taught her the practical skill of basket weaving, which could bring much-needed money into the home. Her father sold the baskets all over Botswana, and she had accompanied him one day on a trip to Maun to sell the baskets to the tourists. It was here she met her husband, Benjamin.

Benjamin had been working in the garage as a petrol pump attendant, not far from where they had set up their stall on the main road. After careful negotiations between Prisca's father and Benjamin, they had got married one year later and moved to Kasane, Benjamin's hometown. Boitachello was born exactly nine months later and, after a very difficult labour and birth, Prisca had been unable to have any more children.

'Where does your husband work now?' asked Abbey, feeling a pang of guilt about not showing more interest in Boitachello and her family.

'He is passed,' replied Prisca quietly. 'I have been on my own for a few years now. I am not interested in men anymore.'

Abbey could see the pain in her eyes and instinctively knew that the scars from whatever had happened were only superficially healed. She wasn't quite sure where Richard fitted into the story, or if he fitted in at all, and she certainly wasn't going to mention his name again. She tactfully changed the subject and talked about the increase in visitors the town was enjoying, and the extra income it brought to the small shop owners, who very often struggled to make ends meet.

After they had finished the second pot of tea, Abbey watched Prisca make her way down the hill and was confident she would be as valuable an employee as her daughter was proving to be. She leaned against the doorframe as Prisca finally disappeared from view. 'Bastards,' she said to herself, when she thought about the contrived plot by Richard and Mr Permelo to lure Prisca into Richard's grimy grasp. A shiver ran down her spine as she imagined what Richard's agenda might have included.

As Prisca disappeared from view, Darren's bakkie swung onto the road at the bottom of the hill. She waited on the porch for him.

'Well, did you find anything out?' she shouted over to him, as he got out the cab.

'I've chased up the complaint at the police station and, to be quite honest, they seem to have several theories how that fire could have started, and none of them include arson. I think they'll pay you a visit though, as I told them I had connections with officers in Gaborone, who would query why so little has been done.'

'What about Richard? Has anyone seen him?'

Darren shook his head.

Richard hadn't been seen since the day he had walked out of the AVP offices. Darren had gone to his house the morning after the fire, but it was empty with no sign of any of his belongings. Mr Permelo had been interviewed by the police at Darren's insistence and denied any knowledge about how the fire might have been started. Abbey could sense Darren's frustration at the lack of police activity, but he had promised not to pay Mr Permelo a visit whilst the so-called investigation was being carried out.

The following weeks flew by as Abbey took up her new position as manager at the office. The regional manager had agreed to increase the Kasane budget to replace the lost stock and help with the repairs. Darren had brought some of his labourers in to help, and the townsfolk also seemed eager to help restore calm and order. Eventually, everything got back to normal and Abbey's small empire was running smoothly again. No stock went missing, no fires were started and Abbey was pleasantly surprised at the number of visits she received from passers-by, who had always wanted to come in and chat, but felt that they wouldn't have been welcome. Abbey quickly capitalised on this and set up a volunteer's notice board and roster for anyone who was interested in helping out.

For the first time since Phil had left, Abbey was starting to feel good about going to work again. She did, however, miss Phil now more than ever. She imagined how well they would have got on running the project together. Abbey was in constant touch with him by e-mail and phone. He had roared with laughter down the line when she had told him about Richard, Mr Permelo and the missing stock. He was also in no doubt about the role Mr Permelo, or Richard, or both, had had in starting the fire.

'Never mind the fire, how are you Phil? Really, I mean, no messing about now?'

'Look, hun, I'm as good as I can be just now. It's taking me a while to get my head around all of this. When you coming back home so I can see you? I really need to talk to you about something.'

'I'm not sure at the moment. Can't you talk over the phone?'

'Nah, no way, not about this.'

'Look Phil, I'll try to get away in the next month or so. It's not easy now I have this place to manage, but as soon as my feet hit British soil I'll be on my way to Sheffield. OK?'

The connection clicked and Abbey replaced the receiver, slightly concerned about what Phil needed to talk about. She doubted very much that getting away in the next six months would be possible.

As well as her work life, married life also got better and better as far as Abbey was concerned. She found she had started to clock-watch at home, waiting for Darren's bakkie to appear on the driveway. When he was away she missed the warmth of his body in the bed and the intimacy they shared. In an attempt to keep him near, she kept the mobile in the bedroom during the night, just in case he managed to get a signal and call.

After one particular lengthy trip, Darren had been away for almost ten days, and Abbey was busy cooking his dinner ready for his imminent return. As soon as she heard his bakkie pull up on the drive, she went over to the door to greet him. He smiled at her and took her in his arms as he usually did, kissing her. He looked tired and sank down into the chair, pulling her onto his lap. She felt his body tense.

'I'll run you a bath,' she said, 'so you'll be nice and clean before we eat.'

'Are you saying I smell?' he laughed.

'Hey, you always smell good to me,' she said, snuggling into his neck. 'No, it's just that you look tired and you need to relax. By the way, you've got at least three messages on the answer phone from the surveyors in Cape Town.'

'Oh,' he groaned. 'I've been expecting this.'

'Anything the matter?'

'It can wait a while. I'll tell you over dinner,' he shouted, as he disappeared into the bathroom.

Darren explained to Abbey over dinner the problems he was facing at work.

'The surveyors are contracted the same way as I am, so they're pushing me for samples,' he sighed, 'and my drilling equipment is fairly dated and not getting through some of the solid layers of rock.

105

I'm literally stuck between a rock and a hard place here. If I don't come up with something soon, they'll cancel my contract and all the money I've invested into this project will be lost.'

'Does that mean you'll be out of business?'

'Probably and there is plenty of competition out there just waiting to step into my shoes. I've been in this business a long time now and I've have built up a good reputation. It's unfair, but I could lose it in a matter of days.'

'Have you any money saved up? Or maybe get a bank loan to buy the new equipment?' asked Abbey trying to be as positive as she could.

'I'm up to the limit with the bank I'm afraid, and no, all my savings have gone into keeping this business going.'

'How much do you need to buy the new drill?'

'Not sure, but probably about sixty thousand would secure a good one. Why?' he looked at her. 'Have you got a solution for me?'

'Maybe.'

Abbey had rented out her small house in south Manchester while she had been away. It had commanded a good rent and was slowly building up a nice little nest egg in a savings account she'd opened specially. This was going to be her cushion when she returned and provide her with cash before the pay cheques started coming back in. She had bought the property over ten years ago and had slowly upgraded it, putting in a new heating system, kitchen and bathroom. She had paid seventy-five thousand pounds for it which, at the time, seemed a colossal amount of money; but property prices in that particular area had rocketed, and she reckoned she could probably sell it in the current market for at least three times that amount, leaving her a tidy profit.

'What if I sell my house?' she suggested.

Darren didn't answer. Instead, he continued to swirl his wine around the glass.

'Well, what do you think? Or at least re-mortgage it?'

'I don't know, Abbey. That's a big sacrifice to make and what if I can't deliver? What then?'

'Well, what's the alternative?' she drove on. 'If we don't raise the money and you go out of business, we're done for anyway. It could mean we have to leave here and try and get jobs back in England. Don't you at least want to give it a try?'

'I'll think about it. Now, no more talk about work, not tonight anyway.'

They spent the weekend relaxing around the house. Employing Prisca had freed up much more time for Abbey, as she no longer had to worry about the cleaning or the washing before Monday morning came round again. Abbey loved spending her weekends with just Darren for company. They took it in turns to cook and spent hours talking over dinner and late into the evening.

It was during these long talks that Abbey learned more about her husband's past as he talked openly about his life. He, too, had got married at nineteen. As he pursued his career, it had taken him away from home for longer periods of time. After one long trip in Namibia, he returned to find the house had been sold and his wife had filed for divorce and had moved in with a man she worked with.

Like Abbey, he had been single ever since and put all his time and effort into building up his business. Abbey got the feeling that Darren firmly blamed himself for the breakup of his marriage, and wondered if she was now benefiting from that experience, as he was the most attentive, considerate man she had ever known.

In the late afternoon, after the temperature had cooled, they walked around the bush land at the back of house, armed with a pair of binoculars, trying to spot some of the colourful birds that nested in the trees and bushes. Darren was quite knowledgeable and was able to tell Abbey the names of most of the ones they spotted, as well as giving her a brief history lesson about the park and its original inhabitants.

She listened as he explained how the San, also known as 'Bushmen', still existed in small numbers, and lived a nomadic lifestyle, surviving solely off the resources the land had to offer. When the Chobe Park had been declared a non-hunting area, the San and other groups of people who had moved into the area had left and spread themselves across the country, mainly in the Kalahari Desert. Then, after diamonds were found in the Kalahari, the San were forced once again to leave their makeshift wooden homes and now lived in resettlement camps, being forced to live off government aid.

Abbey's affection for the country and its people grew stronger as the weeks passed by and, in a bid to understand more fully the culture she was living in, she was keen to learn about its history and traditions. She did, however, feel a great sense of injustice for these indigenous folk, whose own lifestyle and culture seemed to have been sacrificed in the pursuit of riches from gems and the tourist trade. She supposed there had to be losers as well as winners as the country took full advantage of its assets and exploited them to their maximum potential.

'Is there anything we can do to help these people?' she asked. 'Maybe lobby a few MPs?'

'Abbey, take my advice,' replied Darren, 'and say nothing about it publically. This is still a very sensitive situation, and free speech by foreigners about domestic affairs can very often lead to deportation. Trust me on this one!'

The rest of the weekend was spent lazing on the veranda drinking cold beers and trying to keep cool in the shade. Abbey decided not to bring up the subject of money, and would wait for him to instigate the conversation. It was Sunday evening before Darren spoke to her about her suggestion.

'I've been thinking about what you said, and I can foresee a few problems.'

'Go on.'

'Well, this money would have to be on a loan basis only. Second, I can't guarantee repayment quickly. It might take time, depending on the long-term success of the business.'

'I'm well aware of that, Darren, but I want to help and if this is the only way, then so be it. Anyway, aren't we in this together now, as man and wife? If it makes you feel any better, I'll charge you interest. Five per cent above base rate do?'

'Are you completely sure you're happy to remortgage?'

'No, I've no intention of remortgaging. I'm going to sell.'

Darren put down his glass and turned to face her.

'Look Darren,' she continued before he could speak, 'I've decided that if I ever do return to the UK it won't be to that house. We'll buy our own house, together. Somewhere we both want to live.'

He pulled her on top of him, smelling her newly-washed hair, and ran his fingertips across the bottom of her back.

'Can we negotiate the interest rate?' he whispered.

Chapter Sixteen

Abbey spent most of the next week on the phone organising the sale of her house. She instructed the estate agent to give the tenant two months' notice and erect a For Sale board immediately. The house was valued as she had expected, and the agents advised her that, as the market was buoyant, to expect a quick sale. Darren, in the meantime, had driven down to Francistown and managed to raise an overdraft with Barclays of Botswana to cover the cost of the new drill, on the back of the income from the sale of Abbey's house. After a quick goodbye, he packed his bag and left for Johannesburg to buy the new drill, leaving Abbey to sort out any outstanding questions that might come up from either the bank or the surveyors.

Abbey received the first phone call from the surveyors the day after Darren had left, which she didn't think had gone particularly well.

'Hello, can I speak to Darren please?' said the woman in an Afrikaans accent.

'I'm sorry, he's away in Johannesburg on business at the moment. Can I take a message?'

'Who am I talking to?' cut in the voice.

'This is Abbey, his wife.'

There was a moment's silence before the woman spoke again.

'This is Anna Halley from Halley & Gunnell Surveyors in Cape Town. I had no idea that Darren was married - he certainly wasn't a few months ago when he visited us here.'

'I was with him in Cape Town on that visit, Ms Halley. That's when we got engaged.'

'How sweet. Tell Mr Scott I need to speak to him as soon as he returns. He can ring me on my mobile - he has my number.'

The phone clicked and the connection was gone. The abrupt manner of Ms Halley momentarily unnerved Abbey, leaving her feeling quite cold.

When Darren returned at the weekend, he seemed much less preoccupied and suggested they went out for sundowners. This had been one of Abbey's favourite treats since arriving in Chobe and she readily agreed. Sundowners involved driving out into the middle of the bush, late into the afternoon, drinking long, cold cocktails and watching the sunset. They found a shady spot under a large baobab tree and put up the camp chairs. The intense heat from the sun slowly subsided, allowing them to sit in comfort and absorb the sights and smells of the bush.

Impala grazed in the distance unperturbed by their presence. The trumpet of a bull elephant echoed around them, a sign that one of the herds was on the move. In a nearby tree, the sound of the Grey Loerie bird screeched its warning to any game in the vicinity that humans were around, and to be on their guard. The air was completely still and the sky turned into a combination of deep reds and purple as the sun slowly disappeared from view.

Abbey took a sip of her gin and tonic and decided to tell Darren about the phone call from Anna.

'Darren, I had a call after you left from Anna Halley, from the surveyors.'

'What did she say?'

'Not much, although she was quite abrupt and seemed surprised that you had got married. She wants you to ring her back as soon as you can.'

Darren shrugged his shoulders. 'She probably wants confirmation that the meeting is on for next week. I'll ring her on Monday morning. It can wait until then.'

'When is your meeting?' enquired Abbey.

'Next Thursday, in Gaborone. I've organised a project meeting to discuss the findings so far.'

111

'Any chance I could come?' she asked. 'I'm sure I could leave Boitachello alone for a day or two.'

'Of course you can,' he squeezed her hand. 'That would be great.'

Abbey completed as many of the office duties as she could the next week so that there would be very little that might arise. If anything did crop up that Boitachello wasn't sure of, she was under strict orders to wait until Abbey returned and, as she was only going to be away for two days, she couldn't envisage any major catastrophes.

Boitachello, on the other hand, projected an air of confidence as she waved her hand in the air and said, 'Ah, Mma, you worry too much! Everything will be fine.'

Abbey smiled at the transformation from the young nervous girl she had been introduced to a few months ago, to the self-assured young lady she was quickly maturing into.

Boitachello still lived with her mother and, now that they were both in full-time employment, the regular income was having an evident effect on their lifestyles. Abbey had noticed several young men walking past the gate at AVP looking inwards, then turning around awkwardly, before walking back again, hoping to get a glimpse of Boitachello. If Boitachello did notice her string of admirers, she paid them no heed and certainly offered no encouragement. In fact, it had occurred to Abbey that Boitachello seemed to display a certain indifference to men in general, apart from Alfred the volunteer labourer at AVP, whom she scolded more than she praised.

Boitachello's transition had been quite dramatic within a very short space of time. When nobody else was in the office, usually on a Wednesday, which was collection day at the Crossroads, Boitachello would sit on a chair outside the office door under the shading with a cup of tea. She would wave as friends and neighbours walked passed. A few would stop and chat for a while.

112

She loved to people watch and realised that much could be learned about the town and the people who lived in it by simply sitting and observing the goings on around her. She knew which children truanted afternoon study classes and that Pretty, the wife of Moses the mechanic, always had an appointment at the clinic at two o'clock on a Wednesday afternoon. She noticed strangers, faces she had never seen before, travelling up and down the main street on their way to the hotels or safari trips. As she watched the world pass her by, her thoughts often weaved from the past to the present.

Her childhood had not been easy, but she had had the opportunity to go to school, which was more than her mother. She saw education as the key that would open the doors to freedom and independence. She had worked hard at school and left with a handful of Cambridge Overseas GCSEs, optimistic that employers would queue to offer her jobs. After a few months of being told to 'try again next week', the stark reality of being unable to find work emblazoned itself in her mind, and her future looked more uncertain than ever.

Before she got her position at AVP, she had been unemployed for some months, and both her and her mother were struggling to buy enough food. A couple of days after her mother had started work for Mr Morrison, she had come home with a message that Boitachello was to go to his house at four o'clock the next day. Although quite reluctant, Boitachello had duly obliged and Richard had ushered her into the kitchen at the back of the house.

'Ah, yes Boitachello. Now, I'm glad you got my message. I have something very important I wish to discuss with you.'

Boitachello stood silently staring down at the floor, avoiding any direct eye contact with him.

'Your mother has told me that you are not working at the moment. Is that correct?'

Boitachello nodded, still keeping her eyes fixed upon the floor.

'Well, I think I may be able to help you there. You see, there is an opportunity at AVP for a young, strong girl like yourself to come and work for me. Just a couple of days a week to start with, mind. But you never know, it could be more in the future.'

She looked up. Richard's gaze was fixed on her chest. Embarrassed and feeling nervous, she looked back at the floor. She could hear Richard's voice getting closer to her until he was only inches away.

'Actually, we have had a lot of applicants who we really should interview, but I think I could bypass that if I knew for sure that you were interested in the job. Are you interested, Boitachello?'

'Yes Rra, I am interested,' she replied, moving backwards in an attempt to keep some space between them. The kitchen sink blocked her from going any further. She tried to lift her head to meet his gaze. The sickly, sweet smell of recently applied aftershave wafted into her senses as she felt the tips of his shoes make contact with hers.

'Now, I would expect you to show, what shall we say, a small amount of gratitude. I think you know what I mean and you have to realise you are a very lucky girl. There are plenty of young women in this town who would jump at this opportunity. You know that, don't you?' He paused for a couple of seconds before continuing. 'Of course, your mother is also very lucky to have regular employment with me and I know for a fact there are very few jobs around for a woman of her age.'

Boitachello had been expecting this turn of events. It had happened to her before during a brief spell of working in the kitchens at the President's Lodge. She had been sent up to deliver room service to a travel agent from London who was visiting the lodge on a research trip. In order to ensure the hotel was included in the new brochure, the assistant manager had assured the agent that 'all' his needs would be attended to. Boitachello had run out of the room as soon as the man had made clear what his intentions were and reported it to the chef.

She was dismissed within the hour without any hope of a reference. The only way of finding regular employment, without working at the shebeens (where there were always vacancies), would be to leave Kasane and head for the capital. However, the unspoken word is often the loudest and, although her mother had never said anything, Boitachello knew she was ill. Leaving Kasane was not an option in the foreseeable future.

He was now so close she started to feel as though she was suffocating, as if the air in the room was somehow being sucked out. She closed her eyes as he unbuttoned the front of her blouse, pulling it back over her shoulders. She felt the urge to push him away and run out of the door. The memory of the pain from being hungry and the constant search to find food held her prisoner. Her hands continued to grasp onto the edge of the sink, her nails scratching the hard enamel surface. A knock at the front door stopped his advances. He stepped backwards and turned to face the window, now preferring not to look at her at all.

'I will expect you at the office tomorrow afternoon at two, to go over your duties, and back here next week at four o'clock sharp. You can go now.'

Boitachello left by the back door and walked around the side of the house, before buttoning up her blouse. As she walked the short distance back to the small house she shared with her mother, she fought the feeling of nausea, trying to swallow back down the vomit that had stuck in the back of her throat. It was no use - she vomited where she stood.

Her mother was sitting outside in the yard, in the shade, on a small wooden stool when she arrived back home.

'Well,' she asked. 'What did he want?'

'He offered me a job at AVP,' replied Boitachello, trying not to show any emotion in her voice. She felt tears sting her eyes and wiped her face with her sleeve, feigning a cough.

Prisca stared at her daughter for a minute, trying to judge her mood. 'Is everything alright?'

'Yes, it's fine. I start tomorrow.'

Before her mother could ask any more questions, she took the bucket from the outside shed, filled it with soap and water, stripped half naked and washed herself down.

Fortunately, the next week turned out to be very different from what she had feared. The Wednesday she was due to go back to Mr Morrison's house at four o'clock, she had been out with Miss Abbey on her first trip to the Crossroads. She had watched with a combination of admiration and amazement at the skill in which Miss Abbey had dealt with both Mr Permelo and Mr Morrison in quick succession. She had never seen a woman get the better of a man in any situation, let alone two white men who expected nothing but obedience and compliance. Yes, it was true that being white was definitely an advantage; however, she felt there were many valuable lessons to be learned from this woman and, if given the chance, she would observe her more closely in future.

Boitachello had been convinced that she would be fired, now that Miss Abbey knew she had not been interviewed for the job, and she felt too ashamed to explain the circumstances under which she had felt obliged to accept the position. After the shock of being offered a full-time permanent job had worn off, Boitachello was inspired to be like her new boss, and set about creating a totally different person from the shy, nervous young girl who had allowed her dignity to be kicked into the dust.

Prisca also appeared to be much happier than when Abbey had first interviewed her at the house. She would regularly smile and engage in conversation, whereas at first she would endeavour to keep herself away from Abbey and Darren if they were in the house, preferring to keep out of sight, almost as if she felt unworthy to be in their company. This, unfortunately, was an affliction from working for white Afrikaans who still expected the locals to 'know their place'. Prisca had devised her own work routine and Abbey was more than happy to let her get on with her chores in the house in her own way. It had not gone unnoticed by Abbey that Prisca very often went beyond the call of duty and carried out other jobs, like tidying the garden, which she was not expected to do.

Prisca had brought up Boitachello mostly single-handed. Her husband, Benjamin, had struggled to find work in the town and had agreed (rather too readily for Prisca's liking), to hitch a lift out of Kasane to find work wherever he could, leaving Prisca with the responsibility of bringing up their daughter. Apart from the odd letter, she never heard from him. She did her best to provide for her daughter, cleaning houses and weaving baskets, which she gave to one of the stallholders in the town to sell for her.

After weeks, sometimes months, of being away, Benjamin would return with very little money to show for his endeavours. Initially, the disappointment had hurt beyond belief, and she had hurled accusations of drinking and gambling at him. He silenced her grievances with the back of his hand across her face, or the heel of his foot in the small of her back, before taking up his marital rights, leaving her in no doubt of her place within the marriage, and in her husband's mind. Even when she stopped the accusations, he would still get angry and question her ability as a wife and mother, finding fault wherever he could.

The beatings weren't just physical. Benjamin would release a torrent of abuse at both her and Boitachello, systematically breaking down any confidence and self-esteem they had. It was these experiences that Prisca found the most painful. The bruises and black eyes faded, but the venom that came forth from his mouth poisoned her blood, and left her feeling permanently exhausted.

After a few days, Benjamin would disappear from their lives again, leaving behind him yet another chapter of blood and tears. Each night when Prisca went to bed, she prayed for two things. The first prayer was that her husband would never return, and the second, that her daughter's life would turn out to be very different from that of her own.

By the time Boitachello was fourteen years old, Benjamin's trips had become less frequent and his health had started to deteriorate.

117

He spent more time in the house, lying on the mattress on the floor, complaining of being tired and in pain. Despite the constant care and attention Prisca gave him, his condition gradually got worse, regularly coughing up blood and gasping for breath. Each visit to the local clinic resulted in the nurse dispensing two paracetamol tablets and advising him to rest. On the third visit, a doctor finally diagnosed tuberculoses and prescribed anti-biotics. The diagnosis came far too late and the treatment seemed to make no difference. After one particularly acute coughing spate, he closed his eyes and his lungs drew their final breath.

Prisca had walked home from the funeral holding on to her daughter's arm. She knew in her heart the real cause of Benjamin's death had been the disease that everybody was talking about. His long absences had fuelled her suspicions, and when questioned he had never denied sleeping with other women, instead shrugging his shoulders as if there was nothing to explain or justify in his actions.

She also knew that her husband had passed the disease on to her, and her days on this earth were also numbered. Strangely, she felt no bitterness towards her husband, just a sense of peace from knowing that life from now on, although hard, would be more tranquil than ever before. After all these years she was finally free. Her freedom had come at a price, but it was still very welcome.

The regular income from working for Abbey had enabled Prisca to eat a good diet, and her health and her mood were noticeably better. She knew that, once officially diagnosed at the clinic, she would be entitled to the anti-viral drugs paid for by the government, and that this was something she would have to do if she wanted to see her grandchildren being born into the world. The change in her daughter's state of mind and appearance had also given her a new lease of life and the will to live on. Ironically, she felt stronger now than she had done in a very long time.

Abbey Scott was not completely aware of the effect her actions that Wednesday afternoon had had on both these women's lives, and that their commitment to her, at home and at work, was a sign of the gratitude they felt at being released from what they both saw as an impossible situation.

Chapter Seventeen

Abbey and Darren flew down to Gaborone Airport on Thursday morning and took a taxi to the Grand Palm Hotel. The capital of Botswana sprawled out before them as they drove down the dual carriageway on the outskirts of the city. The landline was continually changing, and it was here that the investment into the country's future was really evident. New developments had shot up since Abbey's arrival, consisting of office blocks and shopping malls. The change seemed relentless, as they passed new developments still in the process of being constructed.

The community was also changing, with families moving their homes and businesses from the troubled Johannesburg to the relative calm of Gaborone. Whether the unrest would follow them was a burning question on most people's minds, and crime had definitely taken a turn for the worst. The tense situation in Zimbabwe was also putting a strain on the country's resources, as more desperate refugees arrived in a bid to escape hunger and persecution. Jobs were getting harder to come by, especially for the newly arrived immigrants, and reports of petty crime and burglaries increased weekly as people, desperate for food, took desperate measures.

Despite the significant development, the roads were still busy with a mixture of motorised vehicles, donkey carts, and old-fashioned bicycles. Driving in Botswana was a hazardous and sometimes stressful experience, as etiquette and common sense seemed to evaporate when drivers got behind the wheel and turned the ignition.

The Grand Palm was a prominent landmark on Gaborone's skyline. It was huge hotel, which had developed over the years into a casino, cinema and conference centre. A long driveway lined with palms and grass verges curved its way to the front of the white building. Abbey looked out of the window as the car neared the front entrance. She had spent her first three days in Botswana at this hotel, at a briefing meeting organised by AVP, before all the volunteers had been shipped off to their various destinations.

On the first night, a disco had been organised around the swimming pool so all the new recruits could make contact and socialise. The same evening, the hotel was overrun with American Airmen, fresh from a training exercise in the Kalahari Desert. A swinging party and serious drinking session had ensued. The next morning, after approximately five hours sleep, she had sat at the breakfast table nursing her hangover, when a tall, slim, mousy-haired gentleman sat down opposite her, a huge grin on his face.

'Hell, hun, you look like I feel!'

That was the first time Abbey and Phil met. He spent the next hour trying to be helpful, listing every hangover cure he knew and, although very funny, she was convinced he was making half of them up! Abbey was more than happy when both their names were called out and they were driven to the airport to catch the internal flight up to Kasane. She had known instinctively they were going to get on well.

Darren checked them in at reception as Mr and Mrs Scott, and Abbey felt a warm sensation on hearing these words. This was the first time they had travelled anywhere together since they had got married, and the first time she had heard Darren refer to her as Mrs Scott. He put his hand on her waist as they took the lift up to their room.

'Are you OK?'

'Fine,' she smiled. 'Absolutely fine.'

Abbey did feel fine, but there was a tinge of apprehension about meeting the surveyors at dinner that evening. The phone conversation with Anna Halley was still in her mind, but she had resolved herself not to make any judgements on this woman's character until she had met her in person.

The table had been booked for eight with pre-dinner drinks in the bar. Abbey had brought smart but casual clothes for the evening. At seven-thirty, they walked into the bar and Darren led her over to a table where a man and a woman were already deep in conversation.

The man stood as they approached and Abbey was introduced to Mr Gunnell. Abbey shook his hand, smiled and turned to face his companion who was still sitting down. She took a deep breath as the woman stood up in front of her. She was at least three inches taller than Abbey, and wearing an expensive designer outfit. Her long, blond hair tumbled over her shoulders and Abbey noticed her perfect makeup.

'Abbey, this is Anna,' said Darren. 'I believe you two have spoken on the phone.'

Abbey smiled and held out her hand. Anna responded and shook Abbey's fingers loosely, quickly letting go.

Good grief, that was pathetic, thought Abbey, retracting her hand as quickly as she could. Anna immediately turned to Darren, placed her hands on the top of his arms and kissed him on his cheek, close to his mouth. Abbey pretended not to notice and showed no reaction.

She sat down, picked up the glass of wine that Darren had ordered for her and prayed that the evening would pass quickly. Over the next half an hour, Abbey stayed silent, nodding and smiling in the appropriate places. Her main objective that evening was to scrutinise this woman, who not only dominated the conversation, but who also seemed intent on undermining her confidence.

At five minutes to eight, the headwaiter approached and advised them their table was ready in the restaurant. Anna quickly stood up and linked her arm with Darren's, ushering him past Abbey towards the door. Before Abbey had time to think, Mr Gunnell offered his arm to Abbey. She smiled and took it, thinking it would be impolite to refuse. Darren stood and waited for Abbey to take a seat at the

122

table, sitting beside her. He slid his hand onto her lap, took her hand and squeezed it gently. She looked at him and smiled in appreciation.

'So Darren,' said Anna, without looking at Abbey, 'how is life in Chobe?'

'It's very good,' replied Darren, looking over at Abbey. 'Everything has turned out much better than I could have hoped for.'

Mr Gunnell addressed Abbey directly. 'How do you find Chobe, my dear? Is it to your liking?'

'It took a bit of getting used to, but yes, I am very settled there now.'

'Do you work, Abbey?' continued Mr Gunnell.

'Yes, I work for the charity AVP, looking after the new tree plantations.'

Anna cleared her throat, as if mocking Abbey's statement.

'Of course, I haven't always done that, not that it isn't a good job,' persisted Abbey. 'Before I came to Botswana I…'

'Darren, what's this I hear about a new drill?' cut in Anna, before Abbey could finish her sentence. Abbey drew breath; she was aware her cheeks were starting to burn and quickly excused herself to the ladies' restroom.

Once inside, she leaned on the hand basin and looked in the mirror. What the hell was the matter with her? Why was this woman making her feel so inadequate? She looked at her clothes and wished she had worn something a bit classier. As she straightened her hair in the mirror, the door opened and Anna Halley strode in and washed her hands in the basin beside her. Abbey stood paralysed on the spot; her brain and her body seemed to lose communication. Anna, sensing Abbey's vulnerability, struck quickly.

'So, how long have you actually known your husband, Abbey? I mean, it can't be that long.'

Abbey looked at Anna's flawless reflection in the mirror.

'We've known each other long enough to know that we want to spend the rest of our lives together.'

'Really? Did he say that to you, or you to him?'

'Actually, we both share the same view.'

'You know that's the problem with men, don't you think? They're so, what shall we say, damn predictable.'

'I don't follow you,' said Abbey, her voice still quiet.

'Gosh, you're so naive Abbey, considering your age! I mean in my experience they say what they think you want to hear, while their actions say something completely different. I'm surprised you haven't noticed that!'

Anna looked down at Abbey and smiled before walking confidently out of the room, flicking her head to one side so her hair bounced off her shoulders. Abbey stood completely still. She looked at her own reflection in the mirror. Even with a full makeover, she would never be able to compete with Anna. How could Darren not be attracted to such a stunning-looking woman?

Now she was being silly. Darren had married *her*, in fact he had proposed to her, not the other way around. Those weren't the actions of a man who didn't mean what he said. After a couple of deep breaths, Abbey quickly regained her composure and returned to the table, determined not to let Anna's bullishness intimidate her further.

Dinner finished just after ten and Abbey felt a rush of relief as they said goodnight and retired to their room. As they took the lift, she wanted to speak to Darren about Anna's attitude and the conversation they had had in the ladies' toilet, but felt it should wait until the morning.

Darren appeared completely relaxed and unaware of the inner turmoil going on inside Abbey's head. In a bid to hide her anxiety, she poured him a glass of whiskey, lay on the bed and watched him undress. He smiled and, without saying a word, slid over the top of her, unbuttoning her blouse as he kissed her neck. She had never needed this closeness, this oneness in the same way as she did now.

She encircled her arms around his back, holding on to him, determined not to let him go.

The next morning, Darren was up and showered before Abbey was awake. He had organised a breakfast meeting at eight, to discuss work with Anna and Mr Gunnell, as he hadn't wanted Abbey to feel bored or left out of the conversation the previous evening.

Abbey chose to stay in bed, order room service, and indulge herself with satellite TV. After she had eaten, she showered and made her way to the hotel reception to browse around the selection of shops situated in the reception area of the hotel. She decided to take the stairs rather than the lift, and look at the paintings that were hung around the staircase walls. Abbey smiled at the number of untouched breakfast trays outside doors with the 'do not disturb' sign hanging on the handle. The hotel had been busy last night and she had heard laughter up and down the hallways well into the night.

As she approached the ground floor, she heard Anna's shrill laugh ring out across the foyer. She followed the sound and saw Darren standing with Anna by the reception desk. He was holding a small package in his hand and was showing the contents to Anna. At that moment, Anna turned and spotted Abbey on the stairs. Smiling, and without acknowledging Abbey, she took the box from Darren, kissed him on the cheek and whispered something in his ear which made him smile. Abbey took three steps backwards before turning around and making her way back to the room as quickly as she could. She sat on the bed, feeling paralysed, and once again totally out of control of the situation.

By lunchtime they were on the plane heading for Kasane.

'You're quiet,' commented Darren, after the air stewardess had poured their drinks.

'I didn't enjoy the company last night.'

'You did very well, considering.'

'Considering what, exactly?'

125

'Considering Anna was doing her utmost to wind you up!'

Abbey turned her head to look directly at Darren.

'Why would she do that, Darren? Is it a habit of hers, winding up the wives of her clients, or is there more to it?' She surprised herself at the bluntness of her question.

'It's just the way she is,' replied Darren, ignoring the sharpness in her voice. 'You might have noticed she doesn't like to compete for male attention.'

'And you just play along with her little game, do you?'

'I don't play along at all, Abbey. What's the matter? Are you jealous?'

'No, should I be?'

Darren twisted in his seat to face her. 'Listen Abbey, I think we need to trust one another here. Please don't judge me, based on her behaviour.' He reached into his jacket pocket and handed her a package. It had been exquisitely wrapped. 'I bought you this,' he whispered. 'I hope you like it.'

Abbey removed the wrapping and recognised the box as being the same one she had seen Darren showing Anna earlier. Inside was the carved gold bracelet she had been admiring the day before when they had first arrived at the hotel. Darren slipped it onto her wrist.

Abbey put her arms around him and kissed him.

'I'm sorry,' she whispered before putting her head on Darren's shoulder, squeezing his bicep as if amplifying her apology. He was right. She must put Anna Halley and any silly, insecure thoughts out of her head.

Chapter Eighteen

The smell from the garbage that had being lying untouched for days lingered in the air. Dried fish hung on a wire spanned across the rough ground outside the apartment block. Loud music thumped out of a cassette player, surrounded by a group of young men drinking the local beer. Richard had arrived in the capital after hitching his way down from Kasane. His bank account had soon dried up, due to the fact that the women here wanted more than a promise of a good reference for their services.

In an attempt to replenish his income, he had tried calling at some of the private schools, only to be told the same tale over and over again - there were more teachers currently looking for jobs than there were positions. Finally, he had gone to the Teaching Service Management offices and registered as a teacher for the state schools. As yet, his services had not been required.

Richard had managed to rent a room in a flat near Tlokweng. It wasn't far from the South African border and was one of the poorer areas of town, with rows of concrete apartment blocks. Children and stray dogs roamed the street by day and night. He growled at the children whenever they put out their hands, begging for a few pulas. The clouds of flies made him feel nauseas, as he watched them crawl over the waste that had escaped from the small, corrugated iron shacks, which were used as outside toilets, on patches on waste ground.

At night, he drank in the local shebeens, spending what little hard cash he had left. He was careful not to carry anything of importance, as muggings and stabbings were quite common as people (especially drunk, white people who represented the wealth of the west) made their way home.

He sat at the bar, unshaven and unwashed, pushing away the women trying to force themselves onto his lap in the hope of earning some money. How had he let this happen? How could that bitch have got the better of him? He thought Mr Permelo had said it wouldn't be a problem, and that it was all in hand. He had assured him that Abbey and Phil's future in Botswana was about to come to an abrupt end. The next thing, he had been forced out of his job and out of town under the fear of arrest for fraud. He wouldn't put it past that bitch to turn him in and make even more trouble. He didn't care what happened to her now, as long as it was bad enough to satisfy his revenge.

It was the not knowing that was making him more frustrated. He left the bar, looked around for possible assailants and, sensing it was safe, made his way to the phone box in the next street.

'Ja, Richard. Howz it?' asked Mr Permelo, as if there was nothing wrong.

'It's not,' growled Richard. 'What the hell's going on up there? You said you would get rid of both of them so I could come back.'

'Ja, I know that, but these things take planning and time, you know this. Is it so bad down there?'

'Just tell me what you intend to do and when I can get back up.'

'As you know, part of the plan has already been executed and the other part will be put into place in the next week or two. You're just going to have to be patient with me here, man. I've got my back to watch as well. Don't call me on this number again, unless it's urgent.'

'This *is* urgent,' spat Richard into the mouth piece. 'In fact, it's more than urgent.'

The line clicked dead. Richard, dissatisfied with what he'd heard, pulled up his collar and walked as quickly as he could back to his room.

Not long after their return from Gaborone, Darren left to re-join his team to check on how the new drill was performing. The subject of

Anna Halley had not come up, and Abbey was still feeling uncomfortable at the way this woman blatantly flirted with her husband. No matter how hard she tried to reassure herself, a nagging doubt that there was something she didn't know just wouldn't go away.

Darren was going to be away all week, which gave Abbey time to get up to date with the paperwork that had built up. Boitachello had managed the office very efficiently and Abbey had a pile of phone messages on her desk. The morning flew by as she updated the volunteer rosters and ordered new supplies of saplings.

At lunch time, she decided to walk down to the President's Lodge for a bar snack instead of staying at the office. She ordered her toasties and sat at the same table she and Phil had sat at after their infamous team-building day.

Her gaze wandered across the river and then over to the doorway at the hotel reception. Mr Permelo walked out with another gentleman she did not recognise. He did a double take when he saw her, and stared for a few seconds before taking his companion's arm and walking towards the car park. Abbey gave it no more thought and finished her lunch, relieved that he was on his way out and putting some distance between them. No evidence had ever been found as to the cause of the fire and the police had conveniently closed the file.

That evening, she locked up the AVP plot and walked home, taking her usual route. As she approached the bungalow, she noticed a man in his early twenties standing by the gate, looking towards the front door.

'Dumela Rra,' she called, walking towards him. 'Can I help you? Are you looking for Mr Scott?'

The man did not reply. He half turned to face her, put his hands together as if he was praying, bowed his head and walked away down the hill. Abbey raised her eyebrows at his strange behaviour and thought she would mention it to Boitachello tomorrow to see if she could shed any light as to who he was.

129

Abbey spent the evening reading a selection of magazines and playing with Moxy, Phil's cat, who had decided not to run away and had made herself quite at home. Apart from terrorising the bird population in the garden, she had been a welcome addition to the house, killing insects and chasing spiders.

Abbey decided to try and call Darren to see how he was, but also because she was missing his company. The automated voice clicked in to tell her the number was unavailable and to try later. *Damn*, she thought, *that means no signal, which means I won't be able to reach him all week.*

She replaced the phone onto its cradle. As she did so, something by the bedroom door caught her eye. She walked over and switched on the light. Nothing seemed touched or out of place. She made her way back to the lounge and saw another shadow, this time at the kitchen door. She leaned into the kitchen, stretching her hand onto the wall and flicked the light switch. On first inspection she couldn't see anything unusual. As she turned to go back into the lounge, she saw the shadow again. She walked over to the vegetable basket in the corner of the kitchen. Protruding out from the bottom rack was the unmistakable tail of a snake.

Abbey felt her stomach turn over. She had been in Chobe long enough to know not to make any sudden movements or noise. She also knew that snakes usually only came into houses to find a warm place to sleep when the nights were growing colder, not to attack the inhabitants. She opened the kitchen door to provide an escape route for both her and the snake; then, carefully holding the broom handle, she pulled the vegetable basket away from the wall.

The snake stared at her, raising its head ready to attack. She was in no doubt it was a Mozambique Spitting Cobra, which were highly poisonous. She took a deep breath and, using the bristle end of the broom, gently pushed the snake towards the open door. The snake retaliated, spitting. Abbey stood back, knowing it would try and catch her eyes with its venom. After her second attempt, the snake sensed the night air and slid out of the back door. Abbey ran over and bolted it shut, her heart beating furiously inside her chest. After pouring herself a shot of Darren's whiskey, she carefully checked the rest of the house, looking under chairs and behind cupboards, before retiring for the night.

As well as hiring Boitachello on a full-time basis, Abbey had also employed a labourer called Alfred. Alfred was in his mid twenties and had previously been a volunteer. He had impressed Abbey with his enthusiasm, turning up to help on a daily basis and carrying out instructions to the letter.

Boitachello had seized this opportunity to spend more time working in the office, which she clearly enjoyed much more than working outside, and had introduced some new office routines, which were to be rigorously stuck to. One of the new routines included the favourite national pastime of drinking bush tea. For half an hour every morning at ten o'clock, Abbey sat with her two assistants under the shading outside the office, drinking tea and eating cake. She had decided to buy cakes every morning on her way to work, as an alternative to the Mopani worms that Boitachello always seemed to have in great supply and which Abbey could still not bring herself to swallow, whether they were raw or fried.

At ten-thirty, it was back to work and Abbey smiled as she heard Boitachello exercising her authority over the newly employed Alfred, giving orders to tidy up the yard if she felt he had nothing to do. Alfred was also going to accompany Abbey on her weekly trip to the Crossroads. To her surprise, Alfred declined a seat in the cab of the bakkie, preferring to travel in the back in the open air.

After the trees were loaded, Abbey ate her burger and told Isaac about the snake.

'Did you leave the door open?' asked Isaac.

'No, I don't think so.'

'What about windows?'

'No, and anyway, all the windows have got fly screens on them.'

131

Isaac scowled. 'That does not sound right to me, Miss Abbey. That snake had to get in your house somehow, and if there was nowhere open, I don't understand.'

Abbey had not given any thought as to how the snake had got into the house. She immediately remembered the man standing outside the gate, the same afternoon, but decided not to mention it to avoid any conspiracy theories being created. Instead of feeling better, she now felt a sense of unease at Isaac's suspicion that the snake had not wandered in of its own accord.

'Do you remember when Mr Phil had a snake in his house?' laughed Isaac.

Abbey did remember. They had only been in Kasane two weeks when a snake had visited Phil in his lounge. He had panicked, ran out of the house screaming to his next-door neighbour who, rather worse for drink, had shot at the snake, missed it completely and blasted a kitchen cupboard apart instead. The snake had escaped through the open front door and promptly got run over by a bakkie, as it coiled itself across the road.

That afternoon when she arrived home, Abbey checked all the windows and doors were shut before giving the house a thorough search. The conversation with Isaac had unnerved her and the thought of a snake or baboon spider slithering beneath the duvet in the middle of the night made her feel quite sick. As soon as she was confident that the house was snake free, Abbey settled down to read her book.

She lay on the sofa, casually observing the cat who, in turn, was observing a gecko on the ceiling, which was stealthily creeping up on a mosquito, when the phone rang. Excited at the prospect of speaking to Darren, she ran over to answer.

'Hello.'

'Can I speak to Darren?' came the cold voice of Anna Halley.

'Oh, hi Anna, how are you? Darren's away at the moment, can I take a message?' said Abbey, determined to sound unruffled.

'I'll call him on his mobile,' replied Anna, not returning any courtesies.

'I don't think you'll get him,' said Abbey, 'I've been trying all week and…'

'I think he will pick up for me,' she said, cutting across Abbey once again.

'It's not a case of him not picking up,' said Abbey impatiently. 'It's a case that he won't receive the call!'

The connection had already been severed before she could finish her sentence. 'That damn woman,' she sighed, as she slammed the phone down in annoyance.

A few days later, Abbey arrived at work to find both Boitachello and Alfred standing by the gate of the plot, both wearing very serious expressions.

'What's all this about?' asked Abbey as she took out her keys to open the office door. Neither of them spoke or followed her. Abbey turned around. 'What *is* the matter with you two?'

Boitachello nervously pointed to a small, white package outside the door. Abbey bent over and inspected it before picking it up. As she did, Boitachello began to make a strange clicking noise in the back of her throat and Alfred took a few steps back from the gate.

Abbey removed the white paper to reveal a cardboard box. Inside the box was a small bone. It looked like a small, human finger bone, and Abbey immediately knew what it signified. Someone in the town was letting her know, under no uncertain terms, that her card had been marked, and she was now a target for trouble. She took the box and placed it on the ground outside the gate.

'I'll deal with that in a moment,' she said, motioning to Boitachello and Alfred to come into the plot. They walked forward, cautiously looking at the box as they went past.

Abbey had heard plenty of stories about witchcraft and the traditions that still went on, mainly in small rural communities. Witchcraft medicine, or 'muti' as it was known locally, came from weird and wonderful concoctions of herbs and animal parts. Occasionally, in more sinister cases, it resulted in the death of a child, as the bones and organs of children were deemed to be more powerful in providing a cure for any disease than those of adults or animals. There had been a publicised case in the last few years of a child disappearing in Mochudi, just outside Gaborone, which had been blamed on witchcraft. Unfortunately, no matter how incensed people had been, they were still too frightened to come forward and give evidence, and the case was never solved.

Whenever black magic was thought to be involved, a wall of silence and fear surrounded it. Most towns and villages had a witch doctor and very often they were approached for cures, before doctors and nurses.

The Motswana culture was developing fast; however, black magic was a force that could not be swept away by the introduction of technology or any of the other western ideals.

As soon as Boitachello and Alfred were busy outside, Abbey stole into the office and picked up the phone.

'Hello, Phil is that you?'

'Hi hun, how's it going?'

Abbey gave a deep sigh. 'I think I may have a problem,' she replied. 'A big problem.'

'Go on, spill the beans,' replied Phil, sounding intrigued.

Abbey told Phil about the man outside the bungalow, the snake and now the bone in the box outside the door.

'Wow,' he said. 'Someone's trying to scare you off. Who've you been upsetting lately? Anyone?'

'The only people I can think of are Richard and Mr Permelo, although Richard has left Chobe and the last I heard he was trying to get a job in Gaborone, as a school teacher!'

'You do know that either the AVP plot or you, or both, have been cursed don't you?'

'Phil, this isn't exactly helping to calm my nerves. I rang you for advice, not for a premonition of my death!'

What's Darren said about all of this?' asked Phil.

'Well, that doesn't help either. He's away and I can't get hold of him on his mobile. Phil, what should I do? I'm not even sure whether I should go to the police with this. You know how superstitious people can be here, regardless of who they are and what position they hold.'

'I think you should hide the damn thing, at least until Darren gets back and see if he can sort it out.'

'Good idea, assuming I'm still alive by then!' she laughed, without being amused. 'Where do you suggest I hide it?'

'The corrugated shed at the top of the first plantation,' replied Phil without any hesitation.

'Really?'

'Yeah, there's a tin box hidden in the floor in the left hand corner. Just knock away the earth and you'll find it. No one will look there, I promise you.'

'I take it this is your box, Phil?' she asked. 'And what might I find in it when I open it?'

'Just some weed I had left over.'

'WEED!' hissed Abbey. 'You kept dope at AVP! Good god Phil, you never cease to surprise me, even when you're not here!'

'I wish I was there,' he replied, in a very serious voice.

'Yeah, I know. I'm sorry, that was insensitive of me,' said Abbey, feeling guilty at reminding Phil about his current problems. 'OK, I'll do that and I'll destroy any evidence of your illegal activities too while I'm at it,' she laughed, trying to raise Phil's spirits as much as her own.

'Abbey?'

'What?' she replied, still whispering.

'You could do with finding out who the witch doctor is out there. If he's not involved, then he's your man to sort this out.'

'Oh, well I'll just get the yellow pages should I, and look under W?'

'Tetchy!'

'I know, I'm sorry Phil, but this is doing my head in. I could ask around, I suppose.'

'Abbey,' there was a short silence. 'Let me know how you get on. Promise?'

'Of course I will.'

Abbey took the box up to the shed and found the tin box exactly where Phil had said it would be. She placed the box inside and reburied it. She felt that a casual reassurance to her assistants would not be appropriate and asked both Boitachello and Alfred to come into the office. She explained, in the most confident voice she could muster, that the item had been properly disposed of, all the necessary steps had been taken and there was absolutely no need to worry. She didn't actually know what those steps should be and hoped that neither of them would ask her!

They listened to her every word without any interruption. This was something that people just didn't do in Botswana as it was considered highly impolite. Eventually, they nodded their heads and returned to their duties, Boitachello deciding to spend the rest of the morning in the office, filing and tidying up anything, regardless of whether it was out of place or not.

As Abbey left the office later that morning, she stopped by Boitachello's desk.

'Boitachello, can I ask you something?'

'Yes Mma.'

'Do you happen to know who the witch doctor is in this town?'

Boitachello looked up, her face horrified. 'Oh no Mma, even if I did know, what good would it do? You mustn't ever go and see him. Please Mma, say you won't go.'

'It's OK, I promise, I won't go and see him,' she replied, the fingers of her right hand crossed behind her back. She had done this when she was a little girl, and somehow it always seemed to make lying a bit easier. 'I just wondered who it was, that's all. Please Boitachello, tell me.'

136

Boitachello, unable to say the words, scribbled them down on her note pad. Abbey ripped the paper off the pad before shouting 'Thanks!' and made her way outside.

She sat in the bakkie and carefully unfolded the paper. There were only two words written on it. 'Koma' and 'Limpopo'. Abbey knew there was no use asking Boitachello to explain what she had written and, with Darren not due back for days, there was only one other source of help she could think of.

Isaac was surprised to see her given it wasn't a Wednesday.

'I need your help, Isaac,' said Abbey sipping her coke. 'I think you were right about the way that snake got into my house. I don't think it opened the front door by itself!'

Isaac raised his eyebrows. 'Tell me everything.'

Abbey told Isaac about the man outside her gate as she had walked home, and about the small bone being left outside the office gate.

Isaac's expression was grim. 'I think we have a big problem here, Miss Abbey.'

Abbey groaned. 'That's exactly what I said to Phil this morning, on the phone.'

'What did Mr Phil say?'

'Oh, he told me to hide the bone, which I have done, and then let Darren sort it all out when he gets back.'

'Hmm, that sounds like the most sensible thing I've ever heard Mr Phil say. I hope that's what you're going to do?'

Abbey took the piece of paper from her shorts pocket and handed it over to Isaac. He looked up and shook his head.

'Look Isaac, I know this is a very sensitive subject, but Darren won't be back until the weekend and it might not be a case of waiting for him to come home to help. I might not have that much time. I have absolutely no idea what is going to happen next, and I don't mind admitting I'm a little bit scared here.'

Isaac took her hand. 'I think that's all it is, Miss Abbey. That someone is just trying to scare you away. I don't think your life is in danger, but if you go and start asking questions, and try to find this man, that could change.'

'You know who this man is, then?'

'Yes, I know.'

Abbey left the Crossroads and drove back to town. She pulled over to the side of the road just before the Limpopo Wood Mill, about two kilometres from the centre of the town. This was another example of a successful business, and its proprietor was rumoured to be one of the richest Motswana in the country. He lived with his family in a large bungalow, employed two maids, a gardener and a chauffeur. Abbey suddenly remembered being introduced to a 'Mrs Koma' at the electoral ball. She remembered a tall, well-dressed lady who was pleasant to talk to and who Richard had invited to the office for a personal tour.

She sat and watched as bakkies and lorries, loaded with wood, drove in and out of the yard. She quickly hatched a plan, jumped out of the cab, and walked towards the small office. She could hear voices inside. She knocked and called 'Ko Ko' as she pushed the door. Sat at the desk in front of her was the same man whom she had seen with Mr Permelo at the President's Lodge, a few days before. He looked uncomfortable and stood quickly as she approached him.

'Hello Rra,' she said, greeting him in the traditional way. 'I'm Abbey Scott, from AVP.'

The man extended his arm and returned the greeting. 'Hello Mma, what can I do for you?'

'I'm thinking of building some huts at the plantations and I need to know how much it would cost. I'm sorry Rra, I don't know your name.'

The man looked slightly more at ease with the explanation for her visit. 'My name is Mr Koma. How big are your huts to be, Mma?'

Abbey panicked slightly and quickly blurted out 'Oh... er... three metres by two metres, roughly, that is.' Having learned imperial measurements at school, she hoped that her answer had not sounded too ridiculous.

Mr Koma nodded and Abbey breathed a sigh of relief.

'Come with me,' he replied, and beckoned her to follow him out of the hut.

They walked around the back of the small office to huge piles of wooden planks stored in lines. The labourers stopped what they were doing and stared. Mr Koma shouted over to them and they quickly put their heads down and started work again.

'What sort of wood do you want to use?' he asked, pointing at the wood, but at no particular pile.

'I don't know, Mr Koma, I'm not sure. I was hoping you could recommend the best one.'

Mr Koma muttered under his breath and took a pen out of his pocket, scribbling down some numbers.

'How many huts, Mma?'

'Just the two, please.'

'I will have the wood delivered tomorrow. Should I make the invoice out to AVP?'

'Yes, that would be fine,' cringed Abbey, knowing full well she would have to pay for the wood out of her own money, as any expenses over five hundred pula had to be sanctioned by head office. Not only that, the storage space reserved for the saplings would now be taken up with wood.

'Er, Rra,' she called. 'Mr Koma, please could you deliver to my house? I am short of room at the moment at the office and I have a huge delivery of new trees coming this week. It's the bungalow, at the top of the hill.'

Mr Koma nodded and disappeared into his hut.

Abbey quickly retraced her steps to the bakkie and drove away, her heart still thumping in her chest. *Had that been enough?* she wondered. Would he know that she knew who he really was and leave her alone from now on? Would her visit incense Mr Permelo even further? Time would tell, but at least the wood wouldn't go to the office now, and Boitachello would hopefully be none the wiser to her lie.

She smiled as she drove the short distance back into town. Her experience of meeting the 'witch doctor' was not as she had imagined it. What had she expected? A man wearing traditional dress, living in a cave, sitting in front of a big black cauldron? She guessed that even this part of African culture had moved on with the times.

Chapter Nineteen

The rest of the week passed with no other incidents, although Abbey felt slightly unnerved, and took more notice of who was around her and inspected the house for anything unusual every day. She hadn't heard from Darren all week, and wasn't sure when he would be home. Late that Friday evening, she heard the familiar sound of his bakkie roar up the driveway. He stepped out of the cab and walked over to the piles of wood stacked by the gate. Abbey ran down the path to meet him, throwing her arms around his neck, reluctant to let go.

'Whoa, what's the matter?' asked Darren, hugging her tightly. 'Are we building a new house? Is this one not big enough anymore?'

'God, I've missed you,' she said, as they walked into the bungalow. Once inside, she told him the story from scratch.

'I'll have a word with a few people tomorrow,' he said, a frown forming across his brow, 'and find out exactly what's going on, although I think I already know. I don't know this Mr Koma, but I know he's a crony of Mr Permelo's so that says it all. There's no need to worry, Abbey,' he reassured, 'I'll have this sorted before I leave on Monday.'

'Do you think it'll be as simple as that?' said Abbey, doubtfully.

'Would you prefer me to do nothing?'

Abbey shook her head in an apologetic sort of way, slightly taken aback by his abrupt retort.

'I've been meaning to tell you,' she said, pouring two glasses of wine. 'You know, that Mr Permelo and Richard devised some plot which resulted in Prisca losing her job at the Savuti so Richard could have her working at his house. I hope he never – you know

141

what,' the expression on her face reflecting the disgust at the thought of Richard taking advantage of Prisca.

'Abbey, I honestly don't think Richard had any intention of taking advantage of Prisca. Not when she had a young daughter around who was also in need of a job. Were you there when he interviewed Boitachello?'

'No, Boitachello didn't have...' Abbey gasped, as the realisation of what had happened with her new employee registered in her head. 'I've something else to tell you,' she said. Darren turned to look at her. 'I had to pay for the wood out of my own pocket. I'm afraid I'm eight hundred pula worse off.'

He smiled at her. 'I'll build your huts for you. You may as well have them. That's only if you promise me one thing.'

'What?'

'That you never do anything like visiting Mr Koma again. I know you were worried, but Isaac was right: there was no death threat hanging over you and I think you could have waited until I got home.'

'Going to tell that to the next snake that moves in?' she forced a laugh, but by the expression on his face she could see her comment had hit home.

Abbey rose early the next morning to let in the cat, which had spent the last half an hour meowing and pawing at the kitchen window. She busied herself making breakfast. The coffee pot hissed on the stove and the toast popped out of the toaster, when Darren's phone buzzed on the kitchen table. She picked it up and glanced at the message on the screen. It flashed 'Anna calling'. She deliberated on whether to press the 'reject call' option, but thought better of it, especially after the conversation she and Darren had had on the plane on the way back from Gaborone.

Darren appeared in the doorway, fresh from the shower, towel-drying his hair. She gazed at his tanned torso, as if saving the memory for a later date. He smiled and kissed her, caressing her hair. She rested her head on his shoulder and folded her arms around his back.

'Was that my phone?' he asked, as she poured the coffee.

'Yeah, but I didn't see who it was.' She shocked herself as the lie came effortlessly out of her mouth.

'Listen, I'm going out for half an hour or so,' said Darren, putting his phone into his jeans pocket. 'Make sure you're ready to leave when I get back.'

'Leave? Where're we going?' enquired Abbey, surprised.

'Not telling you, but have an overnight bag ready for the two of us.'

With that, the fly screen slammed shut and the bakkie disappeared down the drive.

When Darren returned, the bags were thrown into the bakkie and they drove south out of Kasane and along the Francistown Road.

'Are you going to tell me where were heading now?' asked Abbey, intrigued by his silence.

'Moremi National Park,' smiled Darren. 'I have a contact there and I've booked us into one of the lodges overnight. I thought a break from Kasane for twenty-four hours would do you good. And, I was hoping it might suffice as a late honeymoon trip?'

Abbey's face flushed with happiness. She put her hand on his arm and mouthed 'thank you' at him.

As they approached the Crossroads, Abbey turned down the radio. 'Can you pull over by the café?' she asked.

'Yeah sure, you needing a comfort break already?'

'No, I want to introduce you to a very good friend of mine.'

Isaac was thrilled when Abbey appeared with Darren in the café. The two men shook hands and, as Abbey had expected, got on very well. Despite being in the same small part of Botswana for the last twenty years, Isaac was knowledgeable and well informed, reading all the newspapers that customers left behind.

'I heard they're coming down hard on immigrants,' he sighed, as Abbey and Darren tucked into their lunch.

'You've been lucky so far Isaac,' said Darren. 'You never know, they might just overlook the fact that you're here.'

'Maybe, but I've been expecting a visit for a very long time now, and I don't fancy being incarcerated in Gaborone Prison.'

'So what's your plan?' asked Abbey.

'Not sure, but I don't own this place. I just sort of took it over from the old guy who gave me a bed for the night and then kept me on serving behind the counter. I'm free to leave at anytime.'

'Any idea who does own it?' enquired Darren.

'No, not a clue. You'd have thought someone would have claimed it by now though!'

Abbey scribbled down her mobile and office number and handed it to Isaac as they were leaving. 'Don't lose touch,' she said squeezing his hand. 'Whatever you decide to do.'

By late afternoon they had travelled the two hundred and twenty kilometres and arrived at the camp in the Moremi National Park. This was a popular tourist destination in Botswana all the year round. Most of the buildings were designed in the traditional African style, with rustic, solid wooden furniture and thatched roofs.

The bedroom was a large canvas tent, which stood high on a platform of stilts, with panoramic views across the landscape. The change in terrain was startling as the still waters of the Okavango Delta embraced the dry and thirsty Kalahari Desert, creating an amazing habitat of unequalled beauty and abundance for the varied wildlife, some of which were unique to this particular part of the country.

Flowers and chilled champagne greeted them as they climbed the steps into their tent.

'Cheers, Mrs Scott,' whispered Darren, as he interlinked his arm with hers.

They ate dinner with Michael and Mia, the camp manager and his wife. Michael was from Cape Town and had met Darren some years before. After several years of managing a backpacker's lodge, he and his wife had wanted a change of scene and taken on the management of the camp. Michael had always kept in touch and up to date with the changes in Darren's life, and was more than happy to accommodate Darren's request. Abbey felt most welcome in their company and was thrilled when her job and the work of AVP dominated the conversation.

'Do you think you're making a real difference up there, Abbey? It's a huge task AVP has taken on,' asked Michael.

'To be quite honest,' she replied, 'I had no idea what I was letting myself in for. You're right though, it is huge task, but that's what I like about AVP's objectives. It's about being proactive and actually doing something positive, instead of just narrating about a bad situation. And, let's face it, we all know actions speak louder than words.' She looked at Darren, Anna's words echoing around her head.

Mia brought her attention back. 'Do you think the Government will have to change its strategy and start culling the herds?'

Abbey sighed and shrugged her shoulders. 'I think they may have to seriously think about it. I just hope it's done humanely, if it has to be done at all.'

She looked over at Darren again. He was looking at her with a soft smile of admiration on his face. Abbey smiled back and the brief feeling of insecurity vanished.

As the evening wore on, Abbey felt herself slowly beginning to unwind. The good company and relaxing surroundings eased the worry of the last week, and any concerns she had brought with her evaporated into the night air. After an outstanding dinner in the small restaurant, they escaped the other guests and sat on the balcony outside their bedroom, listening to the familiar noises of the bush.

That night as she lay with her husband under the mosquito net, Abbey wondered if they would be happy to settle back in the UK and leave behind this lifestyle, which she was rapidly becoming accustomed to.

They made the most of their weekend away and took a trip down the still rivers and open lagoons. A local guide punted their makoro, and Abbey smiled to herself as she remembered the last proposed trip in a mokoro down the Chobe River with Richard and Phil. She lay back and leaned against Darren's shoulder as they meandered through the watery ravines, the feeling of peace and contentment from the previous evening having stretched into the next day. Darren also seemed more relaxed than Abbey had seen him of late, chatting and pointing out the rare birds in the trees and rushes.

The office was dark apart from a low amp bulb burning on the desk. The green leather chair creaked as it turned, partly from lack of maintenance and partly through the weight it was holding. Papers and folders lay strewn across the floor as if thrown from drawers in a hurry. He pulled each desk drawer out in turn, raiding through its contents, looking for anything that could be construed as evidence. He was finding the rage inside of him difficult to contain and, should any unsuspecting employee walk through his door, the sjambok by the desk would get plenty of use.

He knew the police were on their way up from Francistown. An old drinking buddy still on the force had rang him just an hour ago and tipped him off. Damn that English bastard! Him and his bloody wife. They were scum, pond life. Coming here and turning people's lives upside down with their god damn interfering.

A knock on the door broke his concentration. 'Ja, come in,' he shouted.

The door swung open slightly, letting in a shaft of light from the corridor.

'Shut the door, you bloody idiot.'

A short man with broad shoulders and thick arms stood in front of the desk. His afro hair curled tightly against his scalp. On his right hand he wore a gold ring with a solitary diamond in the centre, a trophy from a previous assignment.

'You know the white man – Scott?'

'Ja, I know who he is.'

A piece of paper was exchanged.

'That's the site where they're digging.'

The man took the paper, read it and then set it alight with his cigarette lighter. As the door slammed shut, the bitter-sweet taste of revenge seemed to calm Mr Permelo's fury and he felt able to smile. He looked at the clock on the wall. He had approximately twenty minutes to make his final exit and disappear into the bush.

The weekend passed quickly and, before she knew it, they were back in their bungalow, Darren packing his workbag once again for the next day.

'What about the black magic stuff?' she asked. 'Did you manage to find anything out yesterday?'

'Yeah, I spoke to Mr Kobe and it's not going to be a problem anymore.'

'Oh, why's that?'

'Let's just say Mr Permelo got a visit from the fraud squad yesterday and has decided to go back to Durban and lay low for a while,' replied Darren.

'And Mr Koma?'

'Not an issue anymore.'

Abbey got the distinct feeling she would not get any more information from him and dropped that particular conversation, only to start another.

'Darren, I forgot to tell you. Anna called while you were away last week. Did she manage to get you on your mobile?'

'No, I called her yesterday. I used the landline at the lodge.'

'Oh, you never said,' replied Abbey, slightly annoyed that their perfect day had included a telephone conversation with Anna. 'Is everything OK? With the samples, I mean.'

Darren smiled at her and kissed the back of her hand. 'Everything's just fine.'

'She was totally obnoxious on the phone,' continued Abbey, determined to make her point, and still aggrieved that Anna had been part of their weekend away.

'You should be used to her by now, Abbey. She isn't going to change just to please you. It's just her manner.'

'I'm not expecting her to change to please me, Darren. I just think that she should exercise good manners when speaking to people. It can't be that difficult.'

'Abbey, I think we've already covered this conversation. You're just going to have to be a little bit more thick-skinned when it comes to Anna.'

After a short silence, it was Abbey who spoke next. 'Have you slept with her?'

'Would it matter?'

'I don't know,' she replied, her voice barely audible.

Darren sighed before speaking. 'Yes, I have slept with her. But it was nearly two years ago, well before I met you.'

'Did you have a relationship? I mean, did you go out for long?'

'We didn't go out at all. We slept together one night after a party. That's it, nothing more to tell.'

'Why the hell didn't you tell me?' she said, her voice now raised.

'Because I didn't think it was any of your business,' he replied, his voice also raised.

'Any of my business! I'm your wife, Darren. How could it not be any of my business?'

When Darren spoke to Abbey again it was quietly and calmly. 'Abbey, are you sure you're ready to commit yourself to this marriage?'

'What? Why would you ask that?'

'It's just that you seem hell bent on creating a situation that could destroy it.'

Before she could reply, he got into bed and turned out the bedside light, leaving Abbey sitting on top of the bed in the dark, his comments and her thoughts racing through her mind.

Chapter Twenty

When she awoke the next morning, Darren had already left. He had never left for a work trip before without saying goodbye and she felt hurt, although she knew she had pushed the conversation about Anna too far.

She rang his mobile. 'Hi, Darren?'

'Hi, you're awake. You were dead to the world when I left,' came his reassuring voice.

'Why didn't you wake me?'

'Because I wasn't sure whether you actually wanted to speak to me this morning.'

'That's just silly. I just wish you had told me earlier that...'

The line went dead. Abbey could only assume he had driven into an area with no signal. She threw the phone onto the bed in frustration. He was going to be away all week and she would now have to wait to speak to him at length, and she desperately needed to clear the air.

By the time Abbey arrived at work, the office was already very busy. Boitachello had organised the volunteers that had arrived, and Abbey was impressed with her management skills. Boitachello was proving herself to be an asset in more ways than one.

It was mid morning when Abbey received a phone call from the estate agents in Manchester to confirm they had a definite offer from a cash buyer for her house. The agent was keen to complete the deal and Abbey knew she would have to return home to sort out the house contents, and sign all the necessary paperwork.

'What date are we looking at?' enquired Abbey to the agent.

'Well, this guy is very keen and we really don't want to lose him,' the estate agent explained with an urgent tone. 'The tenant has moved out, the survey has been done and he's already got his end of the conveyancing underway. We can sort out your legal obligations, but you need to empty the house and have it ready for a completion date in the next seven days!'

Abbey sat and thought out her options. She could let AVP know she would be away for approximately ten days, and was sure that Boitachello would be more than capable of managing the office in that time. On the other hand, Darren was scheduled to be away for at least another week and that would mean leaving before he returned. That was something Abbey did not want to do, given the way in which he had left, and also there was no way of getting in touch with him to let him know what was happening.

She decided to take a leisurely lunch and think it over. She walked through the town to the Savuti Safari Lodge and sat in the pool bar. The hotel was quiet and the pool empty. Abbey relaxed into a chair and scanned the menu, when a familiar-looking gentleman approached her.

'Hello Mma, how are you?'

'Hello Rra, I'm fine. And you?' Abbey stood and held out her hand, touching the opposite arm at the elbow, which was customary when greeting someone.

'Fine, just fine. I am Mr Kobe. Do you remember me? I spoke to you and your friend Phil at the Crossroads, when the delivery truck had broken down.'

Abbey nodded. 'Yes, of course I do.'

'I have just been promoted to the post of manager of the hotel,' he continued. 'I know your husband, Mr Scott, and I just wanted to say thank you, and tell you that you are most welcome here anytime.'

Abbey was not sure why she needed to be thanked, but smiled and invited Mr Kobe to join her.

'I am sorry to hear of the very bad things that happened to you, but I think it has all worked out well. Mr Permelo has gone now and Mr Scott gave me a reference when the job came up here. I am very grateful.'

'I am very pleased for you Rra, and thank you for your concern,' replied Abbey, now understanding the situation completely.

'I am originally from Ramotswe,' said Mr Kobe settling himself into his chair. 'When I was younger, I stayed with my uncle and went to school in Gaborone at Ledumang Senior Secondary School. I left when I was nineteen and went to the University of Botswana to complete a Business Management degree. I have been here in Kasane for nearly ten years now and this job has been very good for me. I have been able to help my family, who rely on me for money. The farm has had many problems and they have looked on me to help out.'

They chatted about the work of the AVP and how Botswana's growing prosperity and political stability was helping to create opportunities for its people, mainly by providing schools and colleges even in the remotest parts of the country. Health was still a big problem with the continuing death toll from AIDS, and a high percentage of the population being HIV. However, the government's pledge to invest money into anti-viral drugs and healthcare was a step forward, but they both agreed it had to be recognised as a long-term strategy, not a short-term solution.

It was also very obvious to Abbey that Darren had established himself in the town as a reliable businessman in a relatively short space of time, and was obviously well thought of. She felt a sense of pride that she was connected to him.

'Tell me, Mr Kobe,' enquired Abbey, 'why did Mr Permelo leave?'

Mr Kobe looked surprised. 'Did Mr Scott not tell you?'

'Not really,' replied Abbey, 'I don't think he wanted to worry me. He just said that the fraud squad had been to see Mr Permelo and he had decided to move back to South Africa for a while.'

Mr Kobe laughed. 'Ah, I think it will be a very long, while Mrs Scott. Mr Permelo was involved in trading stolen goods through the hotel here, as well as money laundering. Mr Scott knew all about this and, when he found out what was happening to you, he got

152

written statements from many of us here at the hotel about what we had seen and heard. He faxed them down to the police in Francistown and told us not to worry about Mr Permelo, as now the police finally had some proof about what he had been doing. You know, everyone was frightened of Mr Permelo and he didn't think anyone would ever give evidence against him.'

'Did they arrest Mr Permelo when they came here?'

'No, someone tipped him off, and he ran away, but the fraud squad caught him on the Francistown Road. He was arrested and taken to Gaborone for questioning. As far as I know he is in Gaborone Prison now and will stay there until his court date early next year.'

Abbey smiled with relief. She had dreaded bumping into him in the town, especially if she was on her own.

'Can I ask you another question?' asked Abbey.

Mr Kobe nodded.

'You know Mr Koma, who owns the Limpopo Wood Mill? Is he really a witch doctor?'

Mr Kobe smiled and took her hand. 'No Abbey. Mr Koma is a successful businessman who sometimes uses his position in the town to get his own way. He and Mr Permelo were gambling and drinking partners. They would help each other out of tricky situations. Mr Koma will not cause you anymore trouble. Not now Mr Permelo is in prison. He will not want to risk his name being mentioned in a bad way by anyone. He has a very good business here and has too much to lose.'

Abbey thanked Mr Kobe for his kind hospitality and returned to the office with a plan of action for the next ten days. She booked her flights for the following day and left a long list of jobs for Boitachello, who was overwhelmed with joy when Abbey announced she had to go back home for a week or so and was leaving her in charge. She bowed her head and promised that she would take excellent care of everything until Abbey returned.

Abbey made a mental note to bring both her and Alfred presents on her return.

She walked back to the bungalow and wrote a note to Darren, placing it on the kitchen table, explaining where she had gone and what she had to do. She finished the note with 'I love you', before packing her bag ready for the journey.

Chapter Twenty-One

Abbey landed at Manchester Airport on a chilly, November morning. She took a taxi the short distance to her parents' house, which was about two miles south from the airport. This part of south Manchester was on the border with Cheshire and enjoyed a reputation for being an exclusive place to live. The large houses were set back from the road, behind red brick walls, hawthorn hedges and wrought-iron electric gates. Chestnut trees lined the roads leading into the small village centre, full of trendy wine bars and bistros. Everything looked exactly the same and, although nothing had changed, it felt strange, almost uncomfortable, to be back.

Abbey was feeling slightly apprehensive about seeing her parents again. She had left for Botswana after a particularly heated row with her mother and, apart from a brief phone call announcing that she would be visiting for a few weeks, she had had no other communication with either of them in months. As far as she could remember, she had only had three conversations with her mother since she left over a year ago, and one of those was to tell her she had got married.

'Oh, that's nice,' her mother had said, not indicating any joy or disapproval. 'I'll tell your father when he gets in.' That had been the only response and Abbey had not offered any more information.

She had never had a close relationship with either of her parents, even though she was an only child, and Abbey felt that in her mother's eyes she was still a little girl who had never grown up. She could still tell Abbey what to do and how to do it and she was always right. She viewed Abbey's mistakes, her broken marriage especially, as proof that she could not get things right in her life and that she, as her mother, simply knew best.

155

She constantly reminded Abbey of what she believed to be her failings, forcing her to relive sometimes painful events over and over again. This is what had sparked the row the day before she was due to leave the country. Abbey had called round to her parents' house with some houseplants for them to look after while she was away. She was busily watering them when her mother came into the kitchen.

'I wonder what William would think of this hair-brain plan of yours?' she said, as she tidied away some dishes.

'I take it you're talking about William, my ex-husband of now, let me see, thirteen years ago?' sighed Abbey. 'Who I haven't spoken to since the day we signed the divorce papers.'

Her mother continued to bustle about. 'Well, Abbey, you've never behaved in a responsible way. Your father and I have had a lot to put up with, especially when you were a teenager. I remember you going out and getting drunk and...'

Abbey spun around on her heels. 'How can you throw that at me now?' she cried indignantly. 'For your information, I was pretty tame if I remember rightly. I never did drugs, and I didn't make you grandparents. So I had too much to drink and threw up on the bathroom floor. So bloody what? That isn't so unusual, you know, after a school prom!'

'And, I remember you going out with that awful boy from...' continued her mother, unperturbed by Abbey's sudden outburst.

'MOTHER!' Abbey shouted in desperation. 'Enough is enough. My teenage years are well behind me now. Do we have to go over the same ground, time and time again?'

Her mother stood in the doorway, preparing to leave the room.

'Look,' said Abbey, 'I realise I've made mistakes. OK, I hold my hands up. But I also realise that these mistakes, as you regularly call them, have helped to make me into the person I am now. Isn't that what life is all about?' she paused, twisting strands of her hair between her fingers. 'Do you not like the person I am now?'

She turned around, unable to look directly at her mother anymore and continued to water the plants, hoping and praying that she would get a favourable reply to her last question. She heard the door slam as her mother left the room, unwilling to discuss the matter any further. Abbey left by the back door, tears streaming down her cheeks, knowing that that would be the last conversation she would have with either of them before she left for the airport the next morning.

As she remembered that parting row, it constantly amazed her that she could deal with the most awkward people at work, in a professional manner, and yet two minutes in her mother's company and she immediately reverted into a vulnerable young child. She knew her mother didn't have a high opinion of her, even though she had a successful job and was on the property ladder. God knows what she would think of her now!

The taxi stopped outside 32 Cherrytree Lane. Abbey got out into the wet, chilly air and looked around her. It was all as she remembered it. She fumbled for the front door key in her pocket, turned the lock and walked apprehensively into the hall. Her mother appeared at the kitchen door.

'Hi,' said Abbey, as brightly as she could.

Her mother nodded. 'I've changed your bed and there's a clean towel hanging up in the bathroom.'

'Right then, thanks,' replied Abbey, glad of the excuse to run up the stairs, closely followed by Boris, the cocker spaniel, who was obviously expecting a much bigger greeting at seeing her again than her mother had done.

When her father returned from the newsagents, they sat down to lunch. Fortunately, and much to Abbey's relief, her mother did not ask any awkward questions about why she was selling her house, or about Darren. In fact, her mother didn't ask any questions at all. *Great*, thought Abbey, *she has a new son-in-law and she doesn't even want to see what he looks like or know how he is!*

'Nasty weather,' exclaimed her father as he ate his ham salad.

157

This was the first exchange she had had with him since he walked through the door. Abbey nodded at him, wishing the water in her glass would miraculously turn into red wine.

As soon as the plates were cleared off the table, she text Phil to let him know she was back in the UK and would meet him the following day. After a quick change of clothes, she picked up her coat and the dog lead and headed to the local park with Boris.

The park was almost deserted, which wasn't surprising given the continuous drizzle. She found a bench under an oak tree and sat down. Boris scampered around the trees investigating every smell with his finely-tuned nose.

Abbey was feeling the cold and drew her knees up onto the bench and hugged them. She had played in this park regularly as a child. As she looked upon the familiar surroundings of her childhood, she realised that she had not been homesick at all in the last sixteen months. She also realised that she felt like a very different person to the one that had left that October morning, with a packed suitcase full of what she had considered 'life's little essentials'. Her mind wandered back to Kasane and whether Darren had been home yet and read her letter. She doubted it, as she was sure he would have rang or text her by now, or at least that is what she hoped.

As Abbey sat contemplating, a middle-aged woman shuffled past her and sat down on the other end of the bench. Abbey tried not to stare directly at her, but her shabby appearance drew her attention. The woman was dressed in old, worn clothes with at least three scarves wrapped around her face and head. Her dirty fingers poked through the end of her gloves and her shoes were caked in mud. Wisps of grey hair fell out of the scarves and framed her tired face. Abbey detected a slight odour of urine as she passed by.

'Want a shot?' she said, holding out a gin bottle to Abbey.

'Got any tonic to go with that?'

'Sorry dear,' replied the woman. 'Gave the tonic up some time ago. It kept drowning the gin.'

Now it was the woman surveying Abbey, staring right at her. 'What's your name?'

'Abbey. What's yours?'

'Mary, Mary Jenkins,' said the woman in a very articulate voice.

'Pleased to meet you Mary,' said Abbey, holding out her hand. The woman seemed surprised at Abbey's willingness to interact with her.

'Why are you sitting here, on my bench, in the rain, looking sorry for yourself?' asked Mary.

Abbey winced at her directness. 'Is it that obvious?'

'Guess it's got something to do with a man?' persisted Mary. 'It usually has. Are you married?'

'I hope so. I mean yes, I'm married.'

'Has he left you?'

'No!'

'Have you left him?'

'No, not really. We live in Botswana at the moment and I've come back over to sell my house. That's all.'

'So why the glum face?'

Abbey hesitated for a moment, trying to decide whether she should give out personal information to this complete stranger, who had obviously made a complete and utter mess of her own life. She decided it couldn't do any harm and tried to explain, as simply and as briefly as she could, the strain that Anna's presence had brought on the relationship over the last few weeks.

'It isn't a solid marriage then?' continued Mary.

'Yes, of course it is,' said Abbey, slightly taken aback. 'I love him, he's my whole world.'

'OK, so you don't trust him then?'

Abbey paused and thought for a moment. 'Yes I do, I think. No, I do, completely.'

'Does he know that?'

'No. I mean, I don't know.'

Abbey thought back to the letter she had left. Yes, she had said that she loved him but at no time had she indicated that she totally trusted him, which might have been a good idea, given she had questioned his connection with Anna. She did believe his account that Anna had been a one-night stand; she just hadn't relayed that information to him. Abbey started to feel very uncomfortable and decided to change the focus of the conversation onto Mary.

'So, what about you then?' asked Abbey. 'Why are you sitting here in the rain?'

'Oh, mine's a sad old tale,' laughed Mary, taking another swig of her gin.

'Well, go on, tell me. There must be quite a tale, given your accent is what we would call posh!' Abbey was starting to feel more at ease now and was quite taken with her newfound friend.

'Well, I used to work in London, for a large financial services company. In fact, I ran it. I was the Managing Director for over seven years. We sold mortgages and unsecured loans, and to begin with it was a solid, failsafe business. Our share prices shot through the roof. But, as well as inheriting large profits, we also acquired an inherent complacency about our success. We thought we couldn't go wrong and the risks we took were as big as the loans we handed out. Then, one by one, each debtor defaulted, creditors were down our throat and the business was hanging by a thread.'

Abbey listened in amazement to Mary's tale.

'Was it your fault?'

'Fault wasn't the issue. The shareholders wanted blood, an execution, and it was my head on the block.'

'Did anyone else get fired?'

'Strangely no, just the woman at the top. The Board of Directors all kept their positions, and their pensions.'

'So why are you are here now, like this? Couldn't you get another job?'

Mary laughed. 'No, my name was blacklisted and no one would touch me. I lost my huge salary, my annual bonus and they somehow managed to wangle my pension down to a pittance. I also lost my house, my husband and everything I knew and was familiar with.'

'Why your husband?' asked Abbey, now totally absorbed in the conversation.

'We worked together at the same company. He didn't lose his job and, rather than deal with the initial embarrassment of being married to an ex boss, he exchanged me for a younger model.'

'What about your house? Didn't you make money out of that when it was sold?'

'We should have done, but we took out a second mortgage to pay for our exuberant lifestyle. Believe me, my dear, when I say that our expenses account was nearly as big as our salaries! By the time the house was sold, property prices had dropped in London and we made exactly fifteen thousand pounds, divided by two! So, I came back here to my hometown to try and rebuild my life. Only, I'm just not quite sure how to start.' At this statement, her voice quietened and softened slightly.

Neither woman spoke for a couple of minutes, content just to watch the dogs around the park enthusiastically chase each other around. It was Mary who broke the silence.

'You say you adore your husband and he is your whole world?'

Abbey nodded at her. 'Yes.'

'What was your world like before you met him? How did you view yourself?'

Abbey thought carefully before answering the question. 'I viewed myself as an independent woman - financially, anyway.'

'How do you view yourself now?' pushed Mary.

Abbey started to feel that uncomfortable feeling in the pit of her stomach again. 'I'm not sure anymore. I no longer have a house or a successful career.'

'Do you blame your husband for that?'

'Not really, although I did it for him,' she replied. 'For our marriage, our future.'

'You haven't answered my question. Did he write your resignation or instruct the sale of your house?'

'No, he did neither of those things. He told me on both occasions it was my decision to make.'

'So, why did you do it? Were you trying to make him love you more by sacrificing these things?'

Abbey's mouth dropped. She had never considered this line of thought before. She immediately thought about her father. She remembered buying expensive birthday gifts for him in a bid to impress him and gain his approval. Is this what she had subconsciously done with Darren? Had she sacrificed what she had in an effort to secure his attention, even though he smothered her with love and affection? Was it still not enough?

Eventually Abbey spoke.

'I've been a bloody idiot. I've been so preoccupied with my own feelings, my needs, that I haven't once stopped to consider his. And all the time he's done his best to make me happy and to say and do the right thing.' She thought for another minute. 'You know, I think I've programmed myself to expect failure in all my relationships, instead of building on success. And despite everything, we are a success. *I know* we are. That's why I did it!'

She stood up abruptly, felt in her pocket and took out a fifty pound note.

'Here, treat yourself to a B&B tonight on me, Mary. Oh, and if you ever move on from this bench, you know where to find me.'

Mary smiled and nodded her head. 'I might take you up on that,' she called after Abbey, who was now sprinting back towards the house, Boris racing behind her, his ears flapping in the wind.

Chapter Twenty-Two

When Abbey got home, she made two phone calls. The first was to the landline at the bungalow in Kasane. She let the phone ring for a few minutes before hanging up. She checked her watch. It would be five o'clock in the afternoon in Botswana, so it was still pretty early for Darren to be home. She called his mobile and recorded a voice-mail.

'Hi, Darren, just ringing to check you're OK. Don't know if you've been home yet, but I've had to fly back to England to finalise the house. I'll be back next week. I miss you. Ring me when you get this message.'

The next call was to Phil. 'Hi, listen, change of plan. I need your help to empty this bloody house. Can you come over here, tonight?'

'Of course I can,' replied Phil. 'I'll meet you at Piccadilly Station, in about two hours?'

Abbey grabbed the car keys to her mother's car and drove into the centre of town. She stood by the railings on the platform, waiting for Phil to disembark. She smiled warmly when he came into view, rucksack on his back, walking towards the turnstiles. He smiled back and soon she was hugging him tightly.

'God, I've missed you,' she shouted over the noise of the station. Phil grinned and took her arm as they walked to the car.

'So,' he said rubbing his hands together. 'Come on, I want to know everything.'

Abbey explained on the drive home why she had decided to stay on in Kasane, and the business problems Darren had encountered, hence the sale of her house.

'Hell hun, you must really love this guy to give up everything?'

Abbey twitched slightly, the conversation with Mary still fresh in her mind. 'I do love him Phil, but I think I might have messed up.'

Phil shook his head. 'Nah, from what I know of Darren he wouldn't have anything to do with this Anna woman again. She really doesn't sound his type. I reckon this is a one-way attraction, and if your nerve breaks she'll strike even harder.'

Abbey nodded her head in silent agreement.

'I just wish he'd told me about sleeping with Anna. I feel that she's had one over on me all this time, knowing that I didn't know they had a past, brief as it was. And he doesn't exactly push her away, if you know what I mean.'

'Maybe,' continued Phil, 'his one night stand with Anna meant so little that he thought it wasn't relevant, and that she caused no threat to his future with you. Listen Abbey, for fuck's sake, he's a bloke and she's a good-looking woman. Being in love with you is not going to kill off his ultra male ego! He's still capable of being flattered, you know.'

'Since when did you become Mr Bloody Sensible?' she laughed.

'I always have been,' smirked Phil. 'You've just never appreciated my qualities before!'

They both laughed and Abbey felt calmer.

'If I'm perfectly honest, Abbey,' continued Phil, 'I reckon it's you that's creating a situation that could threaten your relationship with Darren, not Anna.'

Those words reverberated around Abbey's head, as that is exactly what Darren had implied the night before he had left, without saying goodbye.

They spent the evening at Abbey's parents' house watching DVDs and eating Chinese takeaway. Phil introduced himself to both her parents, putting on the most well-to-do voice he could muster. Abbey stood behind them, trying not to laugh. She thought Phil looked well enough, although she noticed he had lost a little bit of weight off his face.

'Are you expecting a call?' he asked, snatching the prawn crackers from her lap, as she checked her mobile for the umpteenth time.

'Yeah, I left a message on Darren's mobile. He's supposed to call me.'

'Maybe he's still out of range? You know how dodgy those signals can be over there. One minute you have one, next you don't!'

'I know, I'm just a bit tense still, that's all, and I really want to talk to him. You're right though, I'm sure he'll ring as soon as he can. Anyway, I've just remembered - didn't you want to talk to me about something you couldn't mention over the phone?'

'It's nothing - or rather, I don't want to talk about it. Not sure it would do any good, anyway. What's done is done.'

Abbey looked at him, a confused look on her face. 'Is that it? Aren't you going to tell me anymore?'

'Your parents seem nice folk,' commented Phil, trying to change the subject.

'Oh yeah, they're nice enough. Just emotionally dysfunctional.'

'What do you mean?'

'Well, I've been home for a whole day, sat and ate lunch with them both, and not once have they asked me what it's like in Botswana, where I live, what my job's like and, more to the point, they haven't even mentioned the fact that I have a husband! It's as though I've been living down the road, and the last sixteen months never happened. I got a better welcome from the bloody dog!'

'Maybe they just find it hard to talk to you.'

'Maybe they just shouldn't have had a child,' replied Abbey with an echo of sorrow in her voice.

'I think being a parent is probably the hardest job in the world,' said Phil wistfully.

'And you would know, hey?' laughed Abbey, startled at his remark.

'Not really. I don't have much to do with Lucy, not now anyway.'

'Who's Lucy?'

'My daughter.'

Abbey looked at Phil with a look of complete surprise. 'You never told me you had a child. How old is she?'

'Thirteen months. I went round to see her last week with a present and she didn't even know me. In fact, she wouldn't come near me. I'm a complete stranger to her.'

'Why, what happened? Have you lost touch with her mother? Were you in a relationship?'

'We were, but after I applied for the job at AVP, Debra accused me of running away from my responsibilities and said that if I went, I wasn't to come back.'

'Were you?' asked Abbey. 'I mean, running away?'

'Yeah, I guess so. It was all so sudden - the pregnancy, and everyone looking at me to do the right thing.'

'And what was the right thing?'

'Getting married and finding a nine to five I suppose. Look, my head was absolute mince at the time and I couldn't think straight at all. I know I've let them down, both of them, but I would like the chance to try and make amends. Be part of Lucy's life. Just in case mine comes to a premature end!'

'I'm not judging you,' replied Abbey. 'I'm in no position to. You don't have to justify your actions to me. In all the time I've known you, you have never judged me and I love you for that. If it's any consolation, I think you'd make a brilliant dad, and I hope one day Lucy makes it happen.'

She squeezed his arm tightly and pecked him on the cheek as she got up to go to bed. She climbed under the duvet, still exhausted from the long haul flight the night before. She checked her phone once more before putting it on the bedside table.

Phil was awoken by the bedroom curtains being opened.

'Come on, sleepy head. We've got lots to do today,' said Abbey, already dressed and ready to go.

They drove to the house and Abbey gave Phil a guided tour.

'Nice pad, Abbey. You sure you want to do this?'

'Yes, I'm sure. Anyway, I can't go back on the deal now - it would leave Darren in a huge financial hole if I did.'

By lunch time, the auction van had loaded the items to be sold, the freight company had loaded the furniture to ship to Kasane, and the local charity shop had picked up anything else. Throughout the morning, Abbey had been checking her phone, even though she knew she would hear it ring or bleep if a text had been received.

'Come on, hun,' said Phil, taking her arm. 'Let's go for lunch, my treat.'

'OK, just give me a minute. I'm just going to try Darren's mobile again.'

Abbey rang the number and it connected immediately. After two rings she heard the unmistakable voice of Anna Halley saying 'Hello' on the other end of the line. Abbey quickly cut the call and sat on the floor, staring at her phone.

She pushed the food around her plate, making no attempt to put any of it in her mouth. After several minutes, Phil broke the painful silence.

'Give me your phone.'

'What?' said Abbey, looking up. 'Why?'

'Just give me your friggin phone. I'm going find out what the hell's happening, once and for all.'

Abbey handed over her phone and Phil walked out of the door, towards the pub car park. After five minutes he was back and handed Abbey her phone. He had a serious look on his face.

'Well?' she almost shrieked at him.

'There's has been an accident. I rang Darren's phone and a nurse picked it up. Apparently, one of the detonators was faulty and the dynamite blew before he had time to take cover. He's in the Private Hospital in Gabs.'

'How bad is he?'

'Not sure, the nurse wouldn't say too much. I had to say I was his brother before I could get anything out of her. He was flown down on Friday afternoon and they operated immediately. He's out of intensive care now, though.'

Abbey sat in silence, staring directly at Phil. Eventually she found her voice again.

'Why didn't they ring me? Why the hell didn't I know?' Her voiced was raised and people started to pay attention.

'They did try to ring you, Abbey. You're the first name in the address book on the bloody phone. You must have been on the plane because they couldn't get through. So, they rang the next number, which was Anna's! She obviously hot-footed it up there, taking advantage of the fact that they were unable to contact you.'

'What am I going to do?' she said in a feeble, almost pathetic voice.

'First, you're going pull yourself together. Then, you're going to ring the airline and get on the next available flight to Gaborone.'

'What about the solicitors, the house and the contract?'

'Abbey, I think there is such a thing as an electronic signature! Now, get on the sodding phone and change your tickets.'

By late afternoon, she had said goodbye to Phil and briefly explained to her parents what had happened.

'I would appreciate it if you could both drive me to the airport,' she said. 'I have to get the five-thirty flight to Heathrow.'

They drove the ten-minute trip to Manchester Airport in complete silence.

'Just drop me at the drop-off point Dad,' requested Abbey. 'There's no need to park up.'

She took her suitcase out of the boot, hesitating momentarily, before hugging them both awkwardly. As they went to get back in the car she turned to face them.

'I'll ring when I get there and let you know how Darren is. Bye then. I love you.'

Neither of them looked up, and Abbey could only assume that they simply hadn't heard as she watched the car drive away.

Chapter Twenty-Three

Abbey arrived in Gaborone and took a taxi from the airport to the hospital. After speaking to the ward sister, the receptionist asked Abbey to make her way to the first floor. The sister was waiting for her as the lift doors opened. She was a large lady with a friendly, smiling face. She held out her hand to Abbey, who shook it in the traditional way and bowed her head slightly, to show her appreciation. The sister led her to a private room at the end of the corridor. Before opening the door, she turned to face Abbey.

'Mr Scott has had an operation. His leg is broken in two places, and he has sprained the muscles in his neck. He was in a lot of pain yesterday, but he is much better today. He has been awake since early this morning and has not stopped asking for you. We have not told him you are coming, so it will be a nice surprise for him.'

Abbey smiled at the sister. She decided not to mention that, as she hadn't rang the hospital to say she was on her way, her appearance would have been a surprise to the staff as well as Darren. The sister was smiling again and motioned to Abbey to enter the room on her own. Nervously, Abbey smiled back and walked into the room.

Darren looked up at her as she walked towards the bed and stretched out his hand. She took it and kissed it, holding it against her cheek, her vision blurred from tears. She leaned over and kissed him on the forehead, stroking his hair. He held the back of her head, pulling her face close to his.

'Abbey, I thought you'd left me.'

'I flew back as soon as I found out what had happened.'

'Flew back! You did leave me!'

'No, you numpty brains. Of course not!' she said, in tears.

Abbey told Darren what had happened with the sale of her house and that she had left him a letter on the kitchen table, explaining where she was and when she would be back.

'It'll still be there,' he replied, 'I never got back to the house. They took me to Kasane Airport and flew me directly down here. Not that I remember much of it. God, it's good to see you,' he said, pulling her in close to him again.

'I left a message on your mobile on Friday, when I got back to Manchester, asking you to ring me.'

'Really? I checked my phone this morning,' said Darren, 'to see if you had been in touch and there wasn't a single message from you!'

'Maybe someone deleted it, accidentally on purpose?'

Darren looked at her, raising his eyebrows. 'Who? The nurses?'

'No. I'm not your first visitor, Darren. When I rang your mobile on Saturday, Anna answered.'

Abbey relayed the story Phil had told her about the hospital not being able to contact her, probably because she was on the plane, and had rang the next number listed.

'Did you know she was here?' asked Abbey, as gently as she could.

'Yes, I knew she was about, but I was that drugged up after the operation, I don't actually remember much about Saturday at all. The only company I've had since then are the nurses and a heavy-handed doctor, checking to see if my head's still attached to my body! Typical of her to jump in though, I suppose.'

'I actually thought I'd lost you,' said Abbey. 'I've been going out of my mind all the way here.'

Darren breathed deeply. 'Listen, I'm sorry I didn't take your concern about Anna more seriously. She is a flirt, I know that, but there is absolutely no chance that she would ever take me away from you, not even for one last fling. I honestly thought you knew that.'

'I know,' she whispered. 'I've not handled this well at all, have I?'

Darren stared at Abbey, as if seeing her for the first time, studying every detail of her face.

'Will you stay here, in the hospital with me? The nurse said they might discharge me in a couple of days, if I'm a good boy,' he grinned.

'Listen soldier, you're not going to get rid of me now. You're stuck with me I'm afraid, twenty-four hours a day until you're completely better!'

'I'm better already, but you can still stick around!'

Abbey straightened the bed for Darren before digging in her pockets for coins.

'Just going to get a coffee. You want one?'

Darren shook his head. 'Don't be long,' he smiled, as she disappeared out of the door.

Abbey found the coffee machine by the front desk on the ward. The nurse smiled at her.

'I think Mr Scott is happy now?' she said questioningly, but as if making a statement at the same time.

'Yes, he is. Thank you.' Abbey put the coins into the machine and then turned to face the desk again. 'Sister, Mr Scott had another visitor on Saturday. A Ms Halley. When did she leave?'

'Ah yes, Ms Halley left as soon as she had spoken to your brother.'

'My brother!' said Abbey, trying not to sound too surprised.

'Yes, he rang and asked to speak to her. I think he told her you would be here very soon and that she could go back home.'

Abbey smiled and decided that Phil deserved a medal for that one.

When she returned to the room, Darren was already asleep. Not wanting to wake him, and completely exhausted after two long haul flights in a short space of time, she kissed him on the forehead and settled down as comfortably as she could for the night. She found some extra blankets in the cupboard under the window, and soon slept soundly in the armchair she had pulled up by Darren's bed.

Darren slept, but kept waking to check her hand was still in his, before falling back to sleep again.

The hospital buzzed with activity, with trolleys and hospital staff continually rushing past the door. Darren and Abbey were engaged in a game of pocket scrabble, when the door opened and a nurse came in, followed by two men in grey suits.

'These are police officers,' said the nurse. 'They wish to interview you.'

Darren nodded and the nurse left, shutting the door quietly behind her.

'We are sorry to bother you Mr Scott,' said one of the officers. 'We appreciate you are still recovering from your accident, but we think we have some important information about what happened. We believe that you employed a labourer called Mani. Is that correct?'

'Yes.'

'How long had he worked for you, Mr Scott?'

Darren furrowed his brow, trying to remember exactly when Mani had started working for him. 'I think it was about three months ago. Is there a problem with him?'

'We interviewed Mani just after your accident and he made a statement which we were happy with. Then, one of my colleagues happened to bump into Mani yesterday in one of the bars in town. The story he told with alcohol inside of him was not the same as his statement.'

Darren pulled himself to the edge of the chair. He had never given a thought to what had happened, other than it was an accident.

The police officer continued.

'We arrested Mani this morning and took him in for questioning. It seems that he was paid to turn a blind eye whilst on night watch, allowing someone to tamper with your equipment, Mr Scott. Obviously, this changes the angle of our investigation.'

'Are you saying this might not have been an accident?' asked Darren, his voice quiet.

'We think that it is entirely possible with this new evidence. The man who paid Mani is known to us. He has always escaped arrest, but we believe he is responsible for several murders in this country.'

Abbey held on to the arms of the chair on hearing this. 'You mean he tried to kill Darren and he's still out there?' she gasped.

'Yes, we're sorry, but we are doing our best to locate him. We suggest that you take great care once leaving the hospital, and report anything you think is suspicious. We have alerted our colleagues in Kasane and they will not only be on the lookout for this man, but will also make regular visits to you both to ensure your safety.'

'What about Mani?' asked Darren. 'What's going to happen to him?'

'Mani has been charged with perverting the course of justice,' replied the second police officer. 'He will go to court next week and can expect a short custodial sentence, and possibly a fine.'

When the police officers had left, Darren pushed away the game with his hand in anger. The small pieces scattered across the floor.

'You know who's behind this, don't you?' he said angrily. 'That bastard Permelo. He knew I'd reported him. Seems I've totally underestimated how downright dangerous that guy is.'

'I think we both did and I sort of feel responsible for this,' groaned Abbey.

'Look, there's no point trying to lay the blame on ourselves here, although I wouldn't mind bumping into Richard,' scathed Darren, 'because if you ask me, he's had a big role to play in this. I bet he had no idea who he was dealing with either, when he got involved with Permelo. In fact, it wouldn't surprise me if they find him all trussed up in Gaborone Dam.'

'My god! Do you think it could be that serious?'

'It depends on how much Richard knows and could tell if they pick him up, which they undoubtedly will.'

Abbey sat quietly, still in shock from the nasty turn of events. There were several unanswered questions about Richard's involvement in a lot of things that had nagged away at her, and which refused to go away. What unnerved her the most was that she had also totally underestimated his contempt for her and perhaps Phil, too. She had a feeling that the situation had still to unfold, and that more revelations and secrets would come out as time went by.

Chapter Twenty-Four

Darren was finally discharged and became the proud owner of a pair of crutches. His care was to be transferred to the clinic in Kasane, who would remove the plaster from his leg in eight weeks time. His clothes had been ripped and covered in blood when he was admitted, and the hospital staff had disposed of them.

'I can't get on the bloody plane in my dressing gown!' he had complained, as the doctor signed the discharge sheet.

She raised her eyebrows. 'I'll sort it.'

Within thirty minutes, Abbey had returned from the shopping mall in Broadhurst, where she had managed to buy a pair of jeans, trainers and a shirt from Woolworths. Abbey presented the nurses with a bouquet of flowers and a box of chocolates, as a thank you before they left for the airport.

The man finished his drink and left twenty pula on the bar. The mall was busy and he felt at ease to wander freely around, blending in with the shoppers. He had not been paid for the last job and it annoyed him. He was always paid, either on delivery or death. This time there had been neither. Scott was not dead. A few superficial injuries maybe, but nothing that wouldn't heal in time. The prospect of being paid at all for his efforts was looking highly unlikely.

Permelo had got himself arrested and his access to any cash had now been scuppered. He had, however, used his 'one' phone call to tell the man that a particular guy had enough information to leave them both dangling at the end of a rope. This guy had lived in Kasane and knew far too much about Permelo's dodgy dealings. The man shook his head at the dangerous lack of foresight of Permelo in allowing this guy access into his affairs.

The man knew that he must find this guy and silence him before the police picked him up. The young man Mani, he had paid at the camp, had been arrested and was now in prison awaiting trial. It was only a matter of time before this guy was arrested too.

He took out the envelope on which he'd scribbled down the address, tore it up and dropped the pieces on the floor. He felt for his passport in his back pocket. After this brief visit into town, the South African border was next on the agenda.

The taxi took them straight to the airport. They queued at the Botswana Airlines Desk, hoping to get a seat on the next flight up to Kasane. They were in luck and, after a few hours' wait, they arrived back at the bungalow by late afternoon. Darren stood at the bottom of the porch steps, leaning on his crutches, and decided the best way to tackle them was on his backside going up, backwards. Abbey giggled at him, and went to help him as he steadied himself back onto his crutches at the top of the porch.

'What the hell?' he gasped, pointing one of his crutches at a small, wooden effigy that was sitting by the front door.

'Do you know what that is?' she asked.

'Of course I do,' replied Darren. 'What the hell is it doing on the porch?'

'It was Phil's idea,' explained Abbey. 'He said a tokalosh would keep the house safe because it's an African devil, and even the hardest criminal wouldn't cross the threshold with that on it!'

'Well, I don't think we'll sack the police quite yet,' he laughed and shook his head in amusement. He had heard the men talk about these things at work, but had never imagined he would have one sitting on guard outside his own front door.

He turned, casting his eyes over the shadows that slowly crept nearer as the light faded, watching and listening for the slightest hint of anything suspicious.

Once inside, Abbey rearranged some of the furniture to give Darren more room to manoeuvre, and moved the rug off the tiled floor to prevent him from slipping and breaking the other leg. The house was clean and welcoming and Abbey's gut feeling about Prisca's reliability had been correct. The white envelope Abbey had left for Darren still sat on the table. She handed it to him. He tore it open and read it.

'I wish I'd got the chance to read this before,' he said sighing. 'I honestly thought you didn't trust me anymore.'

Abbey sat on the arm of the chair directly opposite him.

'Darren, I do trust you and I should have told you that in the letter. In fact, I should have told you that weeks ago. I shouldn't have reacted the way I did. I'm sorry.'

They sat and stared at one another before Abbey broke the silence.

'Do you want me to make up the spare bed for you?' she asked, wearing the most serious expression she could muster.

'You are joking?'

'Well, I just thought you might want the space if you couldn't settle with that leg in plaster!'

'Come here,' he beckoned over to Abbey.

Smiling, she walked over and sat down beside him on the sofa. He pulled her across him. Neither of them spoke, both content just to be in each other's arms, safe and back home.

Abbey returned to work and, true to her promise, Boitachello had everything under control. The news of Darren's accident had spread around the town, and Boitachello looked genuinely relieved to see her and hear that Darren was at home and on the mend.

Abbey suddenly realised that, in her rush to get back, she hadn't bought either Boitachello or Alfred a present. To remedy the situation, she put in an extra one hundred pula in Boitachello's pay packet, and an extra fifty in Alfred's, out of her own money. Their smiles delighted Abbey when they opened their pay packets that Friday afternoon, and were enough to put her in a good mood for the rest of the weekend.

In the week that followed, a constant string of visitors came to wish Darren well. This included Mr Kobe, who arrived with a bottle of Darren's favourite whiskey. Abbey was trying to do a balancing act between the AVP office, attending to Darren and running errands for the prospecting business, and the strain was beginning to show, as she collapsed into her bed just after nine every night.

After Mr Kobe's visit, Darren sat on the veranda looking out across the garden, deep in thought.

'Penny for them,' quipped Abbey, as she came up the steps unnoticed.

'Have you got time to talk?' asked Darren.

'Yeah, I'm on my lunch break to check up on my patient!'

'I spoke to Anna Halley this morning.'

Abbey felt a slight tremor pass through her at the first mention of Anna's name since the hospital.

'Anyway,' Darren continued, 'the samples are in and the reports will be finished by the end of the week, which means that the contract will be concluded as soon as they're passed over.'

'Are you likely to get another one? A contract, I mean,' asked Abbey.

'I don't want another one, Abbey. I've given this a lot of thought recently. I've been doing the same job for nearly fifteen years, and that accident has made me realise there are other things I want to do with my life before I take my final breath.'

'What are you saying? Do you want to move back to England?' she continued in a low voice.

'No, I don't really want to do that either. We're both settled here and I honestly think you will continue to get employment with AVP for as long as you want it. No, Mr Kobe has made me an offer.'

'An offer of what?'

'One of the safari guides is retiring next month and the guy is looking for someone to buy his business. Mr Kobe has suggested that he and I buy it as partners. It has a good reputation, and used by most of the major tour operators as well as being promoted by the

Safari Lodges. He wants to continue as the Manager at the Savuti and I would take on the practical side of running the business, and be the senior partner.'

'How much do you know about running that type of business?'

'Very little,' laughed Darren. 'At the moment that is, but we wouldn't be firing anyone and there is no reason why the business couldn't keep operating as normal. Obviously, I will be learning as I go along, but all the guys know me and Mr Kobe, so we're not unknown entities coming into the business.'

'How much would you need to raise?' asked Abbey.

'Over one hundred thousand pula. I've already had an offer for the new drill, and the other assets in the business from a couple of the other prospectors, so I could raise the capital. But as it's your money as much as mine, I would like your agreement before I do anything.'

Abbey thought quietly, looking out across her garden. She would miss her house, her garden, in fact everything about the place now, and the thought of moving back permanently to England filled her with despair. If Darren bought into the safari business, it would provide them with the opportunity to stay in Kasane for as long as they wanted. The tourist business was booming and, with a little more careful marketing, she was confident it would grow further.

'OK,' she replied. 'I think it's a sound idea and I'm happy for you to go ahead and invest, but on one condition.'

'And what might that be?' replied Darren, slightly bemused at her reaction.

'That you appoint me Marketing Director?'

The police had, as promised, visited them briefly on a daily basis to check all was fine. Although the man they wanted to question still evaded arrest, the officer in charge in Gaborone had sent word that he doubted Darren had anything to worry about, as they had received information that the man had crossed the border into South Africa. Also, because Mr Permelo was now in custody, he was not in a position to be a threat to anyone.

By the end of the month, all the legal work had been completed and Darren had gone into business with Mr Kobe, insisting that Abbey also be named as a partner on the agreement. Mr Kobe had agreed and, with a direct marketing campaign organised by Abbey around the travel agents in Francistown, Maun and Gaborone, the business had increased its profit margin by ten per cent in the first month. Abbey had no intention of giving up her position with AVP, and decided that she could juggle this job with the marketing work she was doing for Darren quite easily.

The week the partnership agreement had been signed, Abbey returned home to find Darren packing a small suitcase.

'Er, what are you doing?' she asked.

'The samples are in and I have to deliver them to the surveyors. I got an e-mail from Anna, saying Mr Gunnell is going to fly up to Gaborone and meet me halfway. I've arranged to meet him on Friday at the Grand Palm.'

Abbey stared at him before replying. 'Darren, your leg is still in plaster and you're on crutches. You can't possibly fly down there, not yet anyway.'

'I have no choice, Abbey. These samples must be in if I'm going to get the final payment.'

'Actually, you do have a choice. I'll go.'

'Are you sure? What about the office?'

'Darren, for Christ's sake, I've left Boitachello for much longer than two days. I think she'll cope without me!'

That Friday, Abbey flew down to Gaborone. She was meeting Mr Gunnell at the hotel at three o'clock in the main bar. She arrived at the hotel at lunchtime and quickly showered before making her way downstairs to the bar. She took a table by the window overlooking the pool. At three o'clock exactly, Abbey looked up to see Anna Halley walk through the door. Anna stopped momentarily as she surveyed Abbey, the expression on her face unable to disguise the disappointment of Darren's absence.

Abbey stood and invited Anna over to the table, before calling the waiter over.

'I was expecting Darren,' said Anna as she took her seat, without offering any greeting.

Abbey smiled. 'He's otherwise engaged, Anna. I take it Mr Gunnell is also busy?'

Anna ignored the question and sipped her water. Abbey, feeling in total control of the situation, took the samples out of her bag and placed them on the table.

'I think you have a cheque for me, Anna?'

Anna picked up the samples and put them into her own bag. 'It won't last, you know,' she said, her eyes not quite managing the same solid stare as on their last meeting. 'This marriage of yours.'

Abbey laughed at her remark. 'Well Anna, what can I say? I've lasted more than one night. But then, isn't that what you're used to? Darren told me about his drunken fumble with you in the dark a few years ago. Unfortunately, he can't actually remember much about it apart from waking up the next morning with a headache.'

Anna stayed silent so Abbey continued, gaining confidence at every turn. 'You're a very attractive woman, Anna. Are you in a relationship at the moment?'

'I don't think that's any of your business,' she replied coldly, now looking down at her knees, not sure how to deal with the backhanded compliment.

'No, you're right, I'm sorry it isn't any of my business. My business is my relationship with my husband. And let me make this perfectly clear to you Anna…' Abbey lowered her voice and spoke slowly, 'Darren is *my* husband. He lives in the same house as me and we sleep in the same bed. Now, is there anything else I can help you with today?'

Without looking at Abbey, Anna stood up and threw down a twenty-pula note to pay for her drink. As she turned to go, Abbey touched her wrist.

'Anna, I think you have a cheque for me?'

Anna took a small brown envelope out of her bag and dropped it onto the table. Abbey watched Anna as she left the bar. Amidst the immense feeling of satisfaction at the way she had handled the situation, she also felt sad for Anna. Sad in that, for all her beauty and money, she was a lonely, insecure woman who couldn't hold down a long-term relationship.

Abbey left the bar, giving the porter the twenty-pula note, and made her way into town to the Main Mall to deposit the cheque in Barclay's Bank.

After her trip, Abbey felt more settled than ever and her normal daily routine soon resumed. One Wednesday afternoon, just after she had returned to the office after her weekly trip to the Crossroads with Alfred, Boitachello ran out of the office waving a piece of paper.

'Miss Abbey,' she shouted, 'Miss Abbey, you have an important phone message. It came whilst you were out and I could not get you on your mobile.'

Abbey took the message and read it. 'What on earth!' she gasped after she had read it for the third time. 'Oh my god, some notice they're giving me.'

The AVP head office had rang to say that they had eventually recruited an extra pair of hands, and the new person would be arriving at Kasane Airport on the afternoon flight. Abbey looked at her watch. It was already two-thirty and the Gaborone flight was due to land in one hour.

'Quick, come with me,' she shouted over to Boitachello, as she sprinted over to the bakkie.

'Where are we going, Mma?' asked Boitachello, who was quite unnerved by the panicked reaction of her boss.

'Look, they'll need somewhere to stay and Phil's house has been empty for months. God knows what's moved in there. We'll need to give it a quick clean. All the stuff we need should be still in the kitchen, or at least that's where I left it!'

Abbey was pleasantly surprised when she went into the house and only found a small army of ants and half a dozen dead cockroaches to clean up. She sprayed the floors with 'Doom' an insecticide spray, which doomed anything it connected with - human, animal or insect. She opened some windows to let in some fresh air and to get rid of the stale smell she had noticed on first entering the house.

Boitachello walked the short distance back to the office and Abbey set off for the airfield. It occurred to her, as she waited in the small airport lounge, that she must look a mess, given she had been moving trees around and sweating profusely in the heat. She attempted to flatten down her hair and wipe away the dark smudges under her eyes, as the small plane landed. She also had no idea who she was meeting. She went over to the administration desk and asked if she could have a piece of A4 paper. She wrote her name and 'AVP' in large black letters and held it up against her chest.

The passengers lined up for the security check before filing into the lounge. Abbey's mouth fell open as the familiar sight of Phil came through the door.

'What the...?' she gasped.

'Hi hun. I take it you weren't expecting me?' he laughed, pointing to the homemade sign across her chest.

She hugged him tightly, smiling at the thought of having her best friend back.

'How did you wangle this one then?' she asked, as they drove back towards the town.

'Well, I decided that given all the adventures you were having, that I was missing out on far too much fun. So, I rang AVP and told them my mother was better and I was free to come out and finish my contract! You are pleased to see me, aren't you?'

'Phil, my darling, do I really have to answer that one?' said Abbey, a smile still beaming across her face. 'What about your prescriptions though? Won't they cost you a fortune?'

'I think,' replied Phil, 'that's a small sacrifice to pay, don't you?'

'What about Lucy? Isn't that a sacrifice too?'

'I tried to talk to Debra, to tell her I was HIV, but I just couldn't do it. She won't let me near Lucy now, and if she knew about my condition, I know she would use it as an extra weapon to keep me at arm's length.'

'That's a shame. I'm sorry, Phil. I really am.'

Phil shook his head.

'She's still hurting, I guess. I don't blame her at all. I left her literally holding the baby. I know her parents have been great and all that, supporting her in all the ways I should have done, but I don't suppose that's been any consolation. No, I'm just going to have to get over it and hope that eventually she'll find it in her heart to forgive me, and let me have some contact with my daughter some day.'

'Don't ever give up on that thought, Phil. Promise me?'

Phil smiled. 'I won't,' he replied. 'I promise.'

Abbey drove Phil straight to her bungalow and sprinted up the steps, shouting to Darren that they had company for dinner. Darren smiled at Phil when he walked into the lounge and shook his hand.

'Welcome back,' he said. 'Now I can share the worry of keeping this live wire in check!' he pointed at Abbey, as she bounced into the kitchen, returning with three bottles of beer.

Abbey smiled and looked at the two men in her life, standing side by side in the same room and raised her glass.

As Abbey prepared dinner, Darren took the opportunity to speak to Phil on the veranda.

'You know, Abbey hasn't once mentioned her parents since she got back from Manchester, and I have to admit I find that kind of strange.'

Phil nodded. 'I met both her parents when she was over. It was really surreal. There are no arguments or anything, and they do speak, but it's always trivial talk, like the weather or what they're going to have for tea. It's weird because you can see the emotion bubbling in Abbey's eyes as if she wants to scream at them, but she doesn't. Instead, she just carries on playing the game and I don't think it'll ever change.'

Darren didn't respond, but looked across the darkness that had fallen over the land, as if someone had suddenly switched off a light.

Phil continued the conversation. 'She was in a dreadful state about you, mate, I can tell you. She thought you'd gone off with that Anna woman.'

'She never had anything to worry about on that score,' said Darren quietly.

'Well, I never thought for one minute the Abbey I knew could collapse into a totally useless heap like that. I'm so glad you guys have sorted everything out. I was really worried about her.'

Darren nodded his head in appreciation of Phil's openness and honesty, but didn't reply.

They ate dinner inside the house and Abbey insisted that Phil stayed with them on his first night back.

'Look Abbey, I'm not a baby,' he said, 'I'm quite capable of looking after myself.'

'I know you are,' she said, slurring her words slightly after three beers, 'but your bed isn't made up and there is no food in your house.'

Phil looked over the table at Darren, who smiled.

'I'd do as I was told if I were you mate,' he said, 'just for today anyway. Oh yes, and thanks to you, we've got a pet tokalosh as well as a bloody cat now. He's called Richard and he lives on our front porch! Feel free to move him into your place, anytime!'

'Oh and Phil,' called Abbey as she stumbled her way to bed, 'Prisca will call in at your house every day for an hour.'

'And who might Prisca be?' whispered Phil, so Abbey couldn't hear.

After a light breakfast, Abbey and Phil walked down to the AVP office. Boitachello and Alfred were already waiting outside the gate. Phil was introduced to both of them and within ten minutes he was sitting behind his old desk, making conversation with Boitachello as she brewed the first cup of tea of the day. Alfred was a little more reserved and drank his tea outside before starting work, occasionally staring into the office to listen in to what was being said.

'Hey, does this mean I get to do the Crossroads trip again?' asked Phil.

Abbey thought for a moment. 'I don't see why not. It'll take even less time with the three of us and more time to eat breakfast and chat to Isaac, who by the way will be thrilled to see you back,' she said, throwing his pen top back at him.

'On a serious note,' said Phil, in a quiet voice so the other two couldn't hear, 'is that tin still in the shed?'

'Oh my god, yes! I'd forgotten all about that. What are we going to do with it?'

'Follow me,' said Phil, and he made his way up the plantation and into the shed. Once inside, he unearthed the tin, took the lid off, and placed it on the ground.

'There is only one way to clear any curse that might be on this,' he said taking a lighter out of his pocket.

'Phil, do you really believe in all this stuff?' said Abbey amazed.

'I'm not sure, but put it this way, hun, I aint about to take any chances.'

He put some paper and some lighter fuel in the tin and set it alight. The tin blazed for a couple of minutes and, when the flames died away, there was nothing left but a blackened tin. Phil stamped on it with his foot until it was flat and then buried it again in the ground.

'Any chance I can move into my house today, or are you going to keep me under house arrest at yours?' asked Phil, as they walked back towards the office.

'Of course you can. Come on, I'll come with you,' replied Abbey.

As they drove the short distance to the bungalow, Abbey asked the question that she had been burning to ask since he got back.

'Phil?'

'Umm.'

'When I got to the hospital, the ward sister told me my brother had rung. What did you say to Anna Halley, just as a matter of interest?'

Phil smiled. 'Do you really want to know? Is it that important?'

Abbey nodded her head vigorously.

'I told her she was an interfering bitch, and that I was on my way over to sort her out. I said, "Abbey may not be in a fit state to deal with you, but I am, and I'm not going to let your evil little games fuck up my best friend's life." Then I told her to get her ass out of the hospital and back to Cape Town before I arrived.'

Abbey looked at Phil wide-eyed, not knowing whether to believe him or not. Whatever he had said had obviously worked and, as far as Abbey was concerned, the name Anna Halley was fast becoming a distant memory.

'Wow, the gate doesn't squeak anymore,' laughed Phil, as he pushed it open. 'What've you done to it?'

Abbey smiled as she watched him walk up the path and through the front door. It felt good knowing he wasn't too far away, for both their sakes.

Chapter Twenty-Six

Phil threw his bags on the coffee table and looked around his house. It felt good to be back and somehow a relief, in that his new lifestyle would no longer reflect the one he had before he left. The house was also very clean and tidy and Phil knew that this Prisca woman would report to Abbey daily, so he would have to make an effort to tidy up after himself. Cold beer, however, was still very much on the agenda and, unbeknown to Abbey (who had left several bottles of vitamin tablets by the kettle), Darren had been in that morning and stocked up his fridge. He snapped the ring pull off the top of the can and put his feet up on the table.

Shadows played on the wall as the sun shone through the trees outside and through the lounge windows. A soft tap on the door broke his daydreaming.

It was Mr Kobe. He came in and sat in the lounge, directly across from Phil.

'Can I offer you a beer?' asked Phil, remembering his manners.

Mr Kobe shook his head. 'I am on my way to work, but I wanted to talk to you about a very delicate matter.'

Phil shuffled uncomfortably on the sofa.

'It is concerning my niece. I think you know of her?'

'Do I?' asked Phil, trying to think if he'd ever been introduced to a Miss Kobe.

'Her name is Ka Ka.'

Phil's heart jumped into his mouth. 'Is Ka Ka alright? I had no idea she was your niece, Mr Kobe.' The words seemed jumbled as they came out of his mouth.

Mr Kobe smiled. 'Nobody knew she was my niece apart from Mr Permelo. She preferred to keep it that way. As to your question, I have to tell you she is passed.'

Phil slumped back into the cushions. He was searching his mind for something to say, but no words came. Mr Kobe, sensing Phil's unease, spoke again.

'Ka Ka died suddenly of a heart attack.'

Phil looked up, slightly confused.

'She was born with a tiny hole in her heart. We have always known about it. Unfortunately, after excelling at her studies at school, Ka Ka decided to spend time going out and socialising with boys. It is much easier to do this in a big city like Gaborone, and the financial rewards gained from this type of activity make it difficult for young women to refuse.'

The realisation of what Mr Kobe was saying started to filter through the confusion in Phil's brain.

'Ka Ka came to Kasane on the request of her family,' continued Mr Kobe. 'They were very worried about her and wanted her to settle somewhere a bit quieter and with fewer temptations. I asked Mr Permelo if he would find her a position at the hotel and he agreed.'

'Did Mr Permelo know about Ka Ka's heart condition?'

'Yes,' replied Mr Kobe. 'Mr Permelo was aware of both her conditions. That is why I needed to speak to you. Before Ka Ka died, she told me that Mr Permelo had paid her five-hundred pula to make your acquaintance. Ka Ka was beside herself with worry and guilt. I think she liked you a lot.'

'I… I... I don't know what to think,' spluttered Phil. 'I have been thinking all this time that I might have, you know, given her...' His voice trailed into silence.

'No, but it is possible that *she* infected *you*.'

Phil thought this was highly unlikely, given the amount of time he had spent in Banjo's bar in the previous months. But still, he wasn't sure and knew he would probably never know.

'For this I am truly sorry,' said Mr Kobe. 'Mr Permelo could be a very persuasive man. I think that Ka Ka was probably frightened for her own safety if she didn't do what she had been asked. I know

191

that doesn't make it right, but I'm just trying to explain to you what pressure she was put under.'

It had been Phil's intention, on returning to Kasane, to visit Ka Ka and either apologise or explain his feelings towards her. He hadn't expected this turn of events and now his redundant, well-rehearsed speech seemed empty and pathetic. He thought about Richard and wondered if he had hated him so much that he had enrolled the services of Mr Permelo to sign his death warrant.

He thanked Mr Kobe for his time and shut the door and the curtains, wanting to block out everything and everyone.

Chapter Twenty-Seven

Phil's return had taken a lot of strain off Abbey, as he knew what had to be done and when. This allowed Abbey to run between the Safari business and the AVP office. One Friday morning, Abbey arrived at the office early, trying to catch up with writing cheques and other duties that Boitachello and Phil were not authorised to do. Phil arrived shortly after eight-thirty.

'You OK?' she asked. She had been aware of his mood swings since his return, and never quite knew what to expect when he came into work.

'Never better, never better,' smiled Phil, filling up the kettle.

He walked over to her desk and looked over her shoulder, pretending to be interested in what she was doing. She giggled and tried to continue, ignoring the silly grunting sounds he was making in a bid to entertain Boitachello.

'Phil, make yourself useful will you and just make the bloody coffee!' she shouted over to him.

Phil's presence in the office had also improved working conditions for Abbey beyond recognition. She had sorely missed the humour and daily banter Phil brought with him, plus the fact he was a dreadful gossip and was full of up-to-date stories on anyone, of any interest or not. He wasn't the most productive of assistants she had ever had, but then he never had been! He was, however, trustworthy and could be relied upon to see a job through to its bitter conclusion, no matter what problems arose.

Boitachello had taken to Phil immediately, laughing at his jokes and quietly ignoring the fact that he paced himself, taking his time to finish his tasks. Alfred had finally overcome his shyness and happily followed Phil around the plantations, a spade resting on his shoulder. Abbey had not told Boitachello or Alfred anything about

Phil's past in Kasane, and had decided that it was his decision to pass on any information, if and when he ever deemed it appropriate. She had also decided not to ask Boitachello about Richard, for fear of resurfacing any bad memories and upsetting her. Boitachello certainly seemed happy enough, and Abbey decided that she was dealing with whatever had happened quite successfully in her own way.

The following week, Phil and Abbey, accompanied by Alfred (who still preferred to sit in the back of the bakkie), drove down to the Crossroads.

'You know, I'm quite excited about seeing old Isaac again,' mused Phil, as he twiddled with the radio tuner.

'He's sure going to get a shock when he sees you,' laughed Abbey, smacking the back of Phil's hand in an effort to stop him changing the station.

They swung into the car park and parked by the door. There were no other cars there, but this wasn't an unusual phenomenon as it could be hours at a time before any vehicles passed by, let alone stopped. It suddenly occurred to Abbey that Isaac led an isolated and quite lonely existence. The café always seemed to be open when she had driven past and she couldn't ever remember him not being there. Phil pushed the door. It didn't move. He pushed it again, this time with his shoulder.

'Bloody hell, it's locked,' he muttered.

He rattled the door handle and they both shouted Isaac's name. Abbey walked around to the small hut she and Phil has slept in the night before the accident. The door was slightly ajar. Abbey called as she walked in. All the furniture was still there, but any personal items belonging to Isaac had gone.

'Phil,' she called. Phil appeared behind her. 'He's gone. I hope to hell he got away in time and they didn't arrest him.'

'Anyway we could find out?' asked Phil.

'Not sure,' said Abbey, shrugging her shoulders. 'I could ask the police in Kasane. I bet they would know.'

The drive back to town was sombre, as the disappointment of not seeing Isaac, and his possible fate, penetrated their thoughts.

Back at the office the mood didn't change as they cleared the backlog of work, which seemed to have suddenly built up.

'Come on,' said Phil. 'I think lunch is in order, don't you?'

Phil could not tolerate morose behaviour any longer than necessary, and was determined to lift everyone's spirits. They were just about to leave, when a tall, sophisticated woman appeared at the door. She was dressed in a light green, linen trouser suit and wore dark glasses that had been pushed up onto her head, keeping her auburn hair out of her eyes. She oozed confidence and dignity as she stood in the doorway, smiling over at Abbey. Abbey smiled, stood up and walked over to the lady.

'Hi,' she said, offering her hand. 'I'm Abbey Scott. Can I help you?'

'You already have, Abbey,' replied the lady. 'It's Mary, Mary Jenkins.'

Abbey stood and stared at the visitor. It couldn't possibly be the same Mary, the tramp Mary, who had spoken to Abbey on the park bench on that cold, wet morning back in Manchester! The voice and the accent, however, were unmistakable.

Mary smiled and took Abbey's hand. 'I owe you a big thank you,' she said. 'And yes, it is me!'

Abbey gasped and shook her hand warmly.

'Well, you did say if I ever moved on from that bench I knew where to find you!' added Mary.

Abbey quickly introduced Mary to Phil, who was mesmerised by the whole situation, and couldn't take his eyes off their visitor. Abbey suggested they went to the Savuti Safari Lodge for lunch to hear the rest of Mary's tale. As Phil drove them in the bakkie, Abbey couldn't help but marvel at Mary's transformation. It now rang true to her more than ever, that appearances could be so deceptive.

Over lunch, Mary began to tell her tale to her captive audience of two.

'Do you remember giving me fifty pounds, Abbey, just before you left the park?'

Abbey nodded.

'Well, that fifty pounds saved my life that day. After I watched you running out of the park, I thought about the question you had asked me.'

'What did she ask you?' asked Phil, concentrating hard on Mary.

'Abbey said to me, "Why are you here now, like this?" I knew I had completely lost control over my life, and my bladder,' she laughed, 'and it wasn't until I saw the determination on Abbey's face to sort out her marriage, that I realised I couldn't just give up on my problems either. I took the fifty pounds, bought myself some delightful new clothes from the charity shop, went to the local swimming pool and got showered and changed. Then, I walked into a solicitor's office, claimed legal aid and sued Leven Financial Services for unfair dismissal.'

'I take it you won?' laughed Abbey.

'You bet I won,' she laughed loudly. 'I was awarded two hundred thousand pounds in compensation, and all my legal costs.'

'Wow, that's fantastic!' swooned Abbey, in complete admiration.

'That's not all,' continued Mary, 'the bastard who was representing the company was only my ex-husband!'

'How did you feel about that?' asked Abbey. 'I mean, about seeing him again?'

'Let's just say that was the icing on the cake!' She paused for a moment. 'I had to come and find you Abbey,' she said, taking her hand. 'I wanted to thank you personally, and to give you this.'

Mary handed Abbey a crisp fifty pound note. Abbey smiled and took it from her.

'Where are you staying?' asked Phil, breaking the silence.

'Here at the Lodge,' replied Mary, waving at Mr Kobe who was busy overseeing the restaurant staff. He smiled and waved enthusiastically back at her.

'That's fine then,' said Abbey. 'Dinner tonight for the four of us. I think it's time you met Darren, don't you?'

Mary smiled. 'I'm looking forward to it.'

'I take it I'm the fourth person?' asked Phil, with a school-boyish grin.

The dinner at the Savuti Lodge that evening was a complete success. Phil and Mary embarked on a verbal sparring match, entertaining Abbey and Darren, who laughed at Phil's resilience to Mary's dry humour, which was mostly directed at him. Mary had dressed for the occasion, and Mr Kobe was more attentive than usual, coming over to check on them at every opportunity, until Darren finally decided to put him out of his misery and asked him to join them for coffee.

'How long are you here for, Mary?' asked Darren, when the table had been finally cleared.

'Well,' smiled Mary, looking at Mr Kobe, 'I was planning on two weeks, but I'm not so sure now.'

'Oh,' said Abbey. 'What do you mean?'

It was Mr Kobe who replied. 'My office manager has had to go to Serowe to look after a sick relative, so I have asked Mrs Jenkins, given her extensive previous business experience, if she would consider helping out until Mma Tau comes back.'

Abbey smiled and clapped her hands together. 'I hope you've accepted, Mary,' she said excitedly.

'Well, let's face it, I haven't got anything to rush back for, and I wouldn't miss out on this for the world,' she said, smiling back at Mr Kobe.

They left the hotel and made their way back home. Abbey and Darren said goodnight to Phil and walked up the hill, hand in hand.

'I think our Mr Kobe is quite taken with Mary,' commented Darren. 'Did you notice the way he kept looking at her and grinning like a Cheshire cat?'

'My god,' replied Abbey. 'She'll have him and Phil eating out of her hand in no time!'

Once inside, Abbey noticed her mobile flashing to indicate a missed call.

'That's strange,' she said checking the call register. 'I've got five missed calls, all from my father!'

Given that her father had never rung her before in her life, Abbey decided to phone immediately.

'Hi Dad, it's me. Sorry for ringing back so late. Is there anything wrong?'

'Yes, I've some bad news I'm afraid,' he replied.

'Oh, what's the matter?'

'She had a pain in her chest and went upstairs to lie down… Anyway, it was quick and she'd gone by the time the ambulance arrived.'

'Who? Who had a chest pain? Dad, you're not making any sense!'

'Mother.'

'Mother had a chest pain? And what do you mean, she'd gone? Gone where exactly?'

'She'd died. She was dead by the time the paramedics got here. I've just told you.'

'What?' Abbey was silent for a few seconds before the words finally came out of her mouth. 'Mother's dead?'

Day and night seemed to merge together for Abbey as she went into a state of shock. Darren quickly organised with Phil to take over at the AVP office, while Mary and Mr Kobe would look after the safari business. Abbey stayed at the bungalow and refused to see any visitors apart from Phil, who sat with her on the veranda. Neither of them spoke, but just having Phil and Darren around her was all she wanted or could cope with at the moment. Darren rang the airline and booked tickets for him and Abbey to fly back to Manchester that weekend.

This time, when Abbey emerged from Manchester Airport, spring was well underway. Flowers and bedding plants were in full bloom in hanging baskets and roadside beds. The cherry blossom stood out magnificently against the blue sky, and the sun shone periodically through the clouds.

A gentle breeze freshened her face as she walked up the path to the front door of her parents' house. Darren squeezed her hand tightly as the door opened and her father stood in front of her. She stood and stared at him, wondering whether or not to hug him. Before she had a chance to make up her mind, he quickly stood aside and ushered them both into the hall.

Abbey introduced Darren and the two men shook hands.

'I'm sorry to meet you under such upsetting circumstances,' said Darren.

Abbey's father nodded silently.

'I'll put the kettle on,' said Abbey, in an attempt to break the tension.

'Dad,' said Abbey, once they were settled with tea and biscuits in the dining room, 'what actually happened?'

'I told you what happened on the phone. She said she had a chest pain and went upstairs. I heard a loud thud and when I got upstairs she was lying on the bedroom floor.'

'I take it she had a heart attack, Mr Harris?' said Darren, trying to help Abbey tease information out of her father.

'Yes, they did a post mortem yesterday.'

'Oh,' said Abbey, shocked. 'You never rang and told me that was going to happen.'

'I didn't think I needed to. It's just routine, you know, whenever anyone dies like that.'

'So, what did they say?' pushed Abbey. 'What did they give as the cause of death?'

'I just told you Abbey, were you not listening? She had a heart attack.'

'But it was so sudden,' said Abbey. 'No warning or anything.'

'Well, considering she had a heart problem, I don't suppose it was that sudden,' Mr Harris muttered impatiently.

'What do you mean, she had a heart problem?' hissed Abbey. 'How long had you both known about this?'

Mr Harris looked uncomfortably at the floor. 'She was diagnosed about three years ago.'

'Three years ago, and you never thought to tell me?' she shouted as she got to her feet. 'Your own daughter, your only daughter and you didn't think I had a right to know!'

'Abbey, calm down,' whispered Darren, taking her arm.

'No, I won't bloody well calm down,' she shouted in her father's direction.

She stood and glared at him, before storming out of the room, slamming the door behind her.

Darren eventually found Abbey in the back garden, sitting on the bench in the sun. He sat down beside her and put his arm around her shoulders.

'Look babes,' he said, kissing her on the head. 'This isn't going to be easy for anyone, and shouting at your father isn't going to put anything right, or make the situation better.'

'I know that, but why do they treat me like someone they barely know? What have I ever done that was so wrong? All I've ever wanted is for them to love me like a normal mum and dad, and do normal things, like go shopping with my mum, spend some quality time with both of them, talk about the things that go on in my life. Is that so wrong?'

'No, not wrong at all. But maybe you're going to have to deal with that later, after the funeral. Your Dad is barely coping himself. You can see that, can't you?'

Abbey nodded. She knew Darren was right, but every time she looked at her father, anger welled up inside of her at his reluctance to show her any emotion, or talk about the sudden loss of his wife and her mother.

Somewhat apprehensive, she went back inside and tried to engage him in conversation, reading the cards of condolence that had arrived.

'Who is this one from?' she continually asked, as names cropped up that she had never heard of.

Her father quickly tired of her questions and, after mumbling his excuses, left the room, leaving Abbey standing alone in the lounge, none the wiser. She looked at the photographs on the wall of her parents on their wedding day, of her grandparents on theirs, and suddenly wondered if, maybe, they had been expecting photographs of her wedding to add to the collection. Apart from a school photograph in Abbey's old bedroom, there was no other proof of her existence in the house.

The house itself seemed to be in a time warp. Nothing had changed since she was a little girl. The same furniture stood in exactly the same place, and the same curtains hung at the windows. It even smelt the same - a combination of furniture polish and a faint odour of over-cooked food.

201

As she wandered around the house over the following couple of days, she felt sadness as the memories of her childhood came flooding back. She saw a little girl with a few dolls, playing in her room, under orders not to make any noise that might disturb anyone, and not to come downstairs until she was called to the table to eat. Meals were always eaten in silence and involved eating off china plates and drinking tea out of china cups. She had been thrilled at being offered a glass of milk, or coke, whenever she was invited to one of her friend's houses for tea. An invitation she was never able to reciprocate.

In retrospect, her parents had never managed to get on the same wavelength as a child, or make any compromises in their lives to accommodate one. She had always felt as though she was in the way, and very insignificant in the scheme of things. It was only when she had started earning her own money that she had taken steps to rectify this in her own mind, as she overhauled her physical appearance with regular visits to the hairdressers, and bought a new wardrobe of clothes every year.

She had watched with envy the clothes her school friends wore, and dreamed of owning a pair of jeans and trainers. Abbey had not been allowed to wear jeans or short skirts, and her attire had caused many arguments in her teenage years as she had tried to leave the house, dressed the same way as her friends.

She had left school at eighteen, just after completing her A levels, preferring a more vocational route than an academic one. Her parents had been dismayed when she turned down unconditional offers from two universities and applied instead for the office junior's position at Paradise Printing. She had married her boyfriend the same year and, when the marriage abruptly ended one year later, Abbey rented her own flat, and embarked on a quest for independence.

Would that have happened if she had been brought up differently? Had her parents been inadvertently responsible for her transition from a quiet, introverted child, into a confident, assertive young woman? These thoughts and many more meandered through Abbey's mind as she tried to make sense of the situation, and take control of her emotions.

Chapter Twenty-Nine

Over the next few days, Darren became an emotional walking stick for Abbey, as well as a means of keeping the peace between her and her father, as they tried to arrange the funeral and agree on what should be included in the service. The night before the funeral, Abbey lay in bed, staring into the darkness, when she felt the need to talk.

'You know, I hardly knew my mother.'

'In what way?' asked Darren, turning over to face her.

'Well, talking to the vicar today for instance. He asked me what her favourite hymns were and I didn't have a bloody clue. I don't know what her favourite flowers were to put on the coffin, and I have no idea about her friends, or who I am going to meet tomorrow at the church. In fact, what *did* she say to her friends about me? Was she proud of me, of who I am, what I'm doing?'

Abbey wondered if she would ever be able to come to terms with her mother's death with so many unanswered questions. Time would tell, but she wasn't optimistic and she wasn't sure she would ever get any answers from her father, who seemed reluctant to talk to her. She closed her eyes, trying to force sleep to come to her, but was still awake when the hall clock chimed three times.

The next morning she was up and showered before Darren was awake. She brought him a cup of coffee and sat on the bed next to him.

'Darren,' she said, kissing him on the forehead. 'I want to go back to Kasane, tomorrow if possible. When are the flights booked for?'

'We're not due to fly back until the weekend, but I can bring them forward if you want. Abbey, are you sure about this? I thought you would want to spend some time at home first, before heading back.'

'This isn't home,' she replied. 'Not anymore.'

Throughout the funeral, Abbey felt she was functioning on automatic pilot. The weather stayed fine and the sun shone, which helped to lift her spirits a little. Her mother was cremated in the village cemetery and Abbey had arranged for a small memorial stone to be placed in the garden of remembrance. On the coffin was a single white rose with a short, handwritten message.

'*Peace comes from remembering that only love is real.*'

This was Abbey's parting gesture to a woman who had played a significant part in her life, and now more than ever she needed to feel at peace from knowing that, despite everything that had happened in the past, her mother did truly love her.

'Be at peace now Mum, please,' whispered Abbey under her breath, as the coffin disappeared through the curtains.

After the service, she played her role as the dutiful daughter, shaking hands with everyone and making polite small talk with some of her mother's friends and a few of the remaining living relatives. A buffet had been organised at a local hotel afterwards, and Darren divided his attention between Abbey and her father, who seemed distant and at times unaware of what was happening. Abbey had managed to get her father's agreement that the flowers were to be sent to a local hospice, and all her mother's clothes were to be collected by the British Heart Foundation, which seemed appropriate given the cause of her death.

That evening, as Abbey busily packed the suitcases ready for their return to Kasane the following day, Darren appeared in the bedroom and sat down on the bed, putting his hand on top of the case, causing her to stop what she was doing. She looked at him quizzically.

'What's the matter?'

'Abbey, you need to talk to your father before tomorrow. You can't leave it like this! Plus, what about the reading of your mother's will? Don't you think he might want your support? Don't you want to know what's in it?'

Abbey didn't reply, but stared aimlessly out of the window overlooking the back garden.

'Look,' pushed Darren. 'We don't need to be at the airport tomorrow until late afternoon, which gives us plenty of time to accompany your dad to the solicitors in the morning. Abbey, I know this is hard, but I think you need to put aside your pain and deal with this as a grown up, instead of a petulant child.'

She turned to face him, the look on her face a combination of anger and pain. Before she could speak, he took hold of her shoulders and looked directly into her face.

'Listen. Before you bite my head off, just hear me out, OK?'

She nodded silently and looked down at the floor rather than at him.

'I'm not saying you have no reason to be hurt or upset with either of your parents, and I think your father is going to have to compromise his position here, although I can now see where you get your stubbornness from.'

'You should have met my mother if you think my father's stubborn!' she whispered, slowly raising her eyes to look at his face.

'Like I said,' continued Darren, 'you and your father need to thrash this out and try to communicate with each other properly. I also think that you have the opportunity to turn this situation around.'

'Oh, how do you suppose I do that?'

'Talk to him, adult to adult, not child to adult. You've complained that they always treat you like a child, so prove him wrong. Your father is only continuing to behave the way he's been programmed to over the last thirty-three years, and if you don't start reacting differently nothing is going to change. Be there for him tomorrow; be calm and, if necessary, take control if he gets upset. You never know, the penny might suddenly drop, and he might start to appreciate you for who you really are. And yes, Abbey, I'm not blind - I do understand why you feel the way you do.'

Abbey stood rooted to the spot. The anger in her subsided and grief immediately took its place. The tears flowed uncontrollably and her body shook as she finally released the suppressed emotion from her system. At no time did Darren try to speak or stop her from crying. He just held her, letting the weight of her body rest on his.

'She never knew,' mumbled Abbey, her head still buried in his shoulder. 'I tried to tell her, the last time I saw her, I tried.'

'Tried to tell her what?'

'That I loved her.'

Abbey agreed to postpone the flights until the weekend. Darren drove the three of them into town for the reading of the will. Her father and the solicitor were the executives and, as expected, everything was to be signed over to her father. Her mother had left Abbey an amethyst necklace, which she had always adored from being a child, but had never been allowed to touch.

'I'd like to have it today if possible, Dad,' said Abbey as they drove back to the house. 'Also, can I have a look through some of the family photographs, and maybe take some of the three of us back with me?'

Her father nodded absently in the back of the car but made no reply, preferring to look out of the car window and not in the direction of Abbey, who had turned around to face him.

At midday the following Saturday, the suitcases stood ready in the hall. Darren had booked a taxi back to the airport. Abbey was sitting in the dining room, going through a box of photographs that her father had eventually and very reluctantly retrieved from the attic. She put a couple into her bag and couldn't help but think there were very few of her as a young child, or any family portraits. She comforted herself with the thought that maybe that sort of thing just wasn't done when she was growing up. Yes, she was sure that would be the reason.

'Abbey, the taxi will be here soon. Are you ready to go?' called Darren, who was standing in the doorway holding her jacket.

'OK, just coming. Dad, did you find the necklace for me?' she shouted up the stairs.

Her father appeared on the landing.

'I put it in an envelope, on the table. Didn't you see it?'

Abbey walked over to the table, picked up a plain brown envelope and looked inside. She slowly turned to face her father and held the envelope out to him.

'I want you to give this necklace to me,' she whispered.

'I don't understand,' he said quietly. 'You already have it.'

Abbey repeated her request, her heart now thumping inside her chest.

'Dad, I want you to take the necklace out of this envelope and hand it to me personally. You haven't even written my name on the front. This necklace is a gift from my mother, not a letter from a stranger to be left on the table without a word, in the hope that I might just notice it!'

He stared at her, looking slightly confused. He then took the envelope and handed her the necklace.

'Thank you.' She took the necklace, aware that her hand was shaking. 'Dad, I know this is hard,' she continued, determined not to let this opportunity slip by, 'but you don't have to be so guarded anymore in what you say or think. In fact, you're going to have to start thinking for yourself again and make your own decisions.'

He stood fumbling in his pockets, not once looking at his daughter.

'And,' she took a deep breath, 'I was hoping that you and I could maybe start again? It's not too late, you know. It's never too late.'

His head slowly turned. His face was ashen grey and, as Abbey looked into his eyes, she got the distinct feeling that an inner struggle was going on inside.

'Look, I've no intention of walking away from you. This isn't the end,' she said quietly. 'This is the beginning of a new era, for both of us.'

She walked towards Darren, and looked back at her father. 'Oh, and Dad, I love you. Just so you know.'

They drove to the airport, Abbey finally with a sense of peace that had eluded her since the disjointed phone call from her father informing her of her mother's death. Darren sat close to her with his arm around her shoulder.

'I'm so proud of you Abbey, I really am. I know how difficult that must have been for you.'

'I know this sounds awful,' she replied, 'but when I think about it, he's never had the opportunity to express his feelings, or become the person he had the potential to be, and perhaps still could be. It's like he's been cocooned, not really living, if you know what I mean. In fact, they both have. They created an existence that not only seemed to stifle them emotionally, but actually encouraged them to behave in quite a destructive way.'

The tree-lined roads and gardens flashed past outside the car window.

'Do you think what I said to him will do any good and he'll keep in touch?'

'We'll make sure of it. But like you said, this isn't the end, it's a new beginning.'

She placed her hand on his arm. 'Thank you,' she said. 'For everything,' and kissed him on the cheek.

Chapter Thirty

Abbey descended down the steps of the small Botswana aircraft and onto the runway at Kasane Airport, looking around at the expanse of wilderness. The heat and the dust seemed to envelop them as they walked towards the airport building; but rather than it being uncomfortable, it gave her a feeling of familiarity, of being back home. Phil had driven Darren's bakkie up and was waiting for them in the airport car park, leaning against the cab, smoking a cigarette.

'Home James,' joked Abbey, after the bags had been thrown in the back. She looked out of the window as they made their way towards the town. She felt excited to be back amongst people she knew, and smiled to herself as they drove up to the bungalow.

'I'll walk back,' said Phil, throwing the keys to Darren. 'And, I'll catch up with you both tomorrow, not that you've missed much. Although!' he paused for a second. 'Nah,' he laughed, 'it can wait.' He waved and disappeared down the drive.

Abbey was about to embark up the front steps when Darren took her arm.

'I think Mrs Scott,' he said, 'there is something I have omitted to do.'

'Oh, and what might that be, Mr Scott?'

He scooped her up into his arms and carried her over the threshold into the lounge. She giggled as he put her down, falling onto the sofa, feigning breathlessness. She looked around her house. Everywhere was spotless and there was a huge bouquet of flowers, beautifully arranged in a vase on the table. Abbey had a sneaking suspicion that Mary had been behind that idea.

She walked out onto the veranda and surveyed her garden and beyond. Darren came out and stood by her side, putting his arm around her waist. The sky blackened and large raindrops started to fall onto the parched ground. Abbey breathed in the cool, refreshed air.

'Put your shoes back on,' said Darren suddenly.

'What? What for?'

'Honestly woman, will you ever just do as you're told without holding a judicial review?'

Abbey laughed, slipped her sandals back on and followed Darren to the bakkie. They drove out of town along the familiar road, heading south, the heavy rain splashing onto the windscreen.

'Darren, are you going to tell me where we're going?'

'No, is the simple answer to that.'

As the bakkie approached the Crossroads, Darren pulled over into the café car park.

'Why on earth are we here?' she asked, jumping down out of the cab. Without answering, he took her hand and led her to the door. She looked at him puzzled.

'Open it.'

'What?'

'Abbey, open the door.'

She opened the door and walked inside. The cheers and laughter nearly knocked her off her feet. The room was full of people. Mr Kobe, Phil, Boitachello, Mary, Alfred and lots of other faces she knew from the town.

Behind the counter stood Isaac, a huge smile lighting up his face. Abbey ran over to him and hugged him.

'My god Isaac, where you've been?' she asked, half laughing, half crying.

'They got me Miss Abbey, they came for me. I knew they would.'

'Is everything OK? Are you going to have to go back to Zim?'

'No, and thanks to your husband, you're going to have to eat my burgers for some time yet!'

Abbey looked around the café. It had been painted and the furniture had been replaced. She took Darren's arm and led him to an unoccupied table.

'How?' she said looking at him.

'After you told me what had happened to Isaac,' replied Darren, 'I went to see Sergeant Lephepe in Kasane. I knew you had enough on your mind after the news about your mother. Anyway, he found out Isaac had been taken to Francistown and was being held there whilst the police waited for a deportation order. I enlisted Mr Kobe's help and sent him with some money and told him to take Isaac back to the hotel. They arrived in Kasane just after we had left for your parents' house. Whilst we were away, I made a few phone calls and found out who this place belongs to. Apparently, it's on the deeds of the Savuti Lodge, which essentially means it's in Mr Kobe's hands.'

'Does this mean Isaac can stay? I mean in Botswana, legally?'

Darren nodded. 'Yes. Mr Kobe appointed Isaac as the café manager and has given him a written contract. That means he can apply for a resident's permit now. Not only that, but Mr Kobe decided that this café could be a thriving business and an asset to the hotel. He has invested money modernising it, including all the kitchen equipment.'

Abbey stared at her husband. 'You know, you never cease to amaze me! Just when I think I know you, you go and do something else that makes me realise I still have so much to learn.' She made her way around the table and sat on his lap. 'Mr Scott,' she said, putting her arms around his neck. 'Will you marry me?'

Darren looked back at her, slightly confused. 'Aren't we already married?'

'Well yes, but I want to get married again. This time in Kasane, at the church, with all these people present.'

Darren smiled. 'Oh course I'll marry you, Mrs Scott. It would be an honour.'

They arranged to get married, again, two weeks later in the small church in the town. Darren's family flew over from New Zealand, as they were determined not to miss out second time around. They had been booked into the Savuti Lodge at the personal invitation of Mr Kobe. Darren and Abbey decided to stay at the bungalow and sleep in the same bed, ignoring any superstition about the groom seeing the bride the night before the wedding. Phil arranged a quiet, or so he promised, stag night at the President's Lodge, and Mary invited all the ladies to a BBQ at the house she was renting in the town.

Despite the fact Abbey was already married to Darren and had been so for some months, she could not remember being so excited or nervous. She remembered the short ceremony in Francistown where they first got married without one invited guest, and the drive back to the bungalow the same day.

As she sat daydreaming in the garden at Mary's house, she felt a hand touch her on the shoulder. Darren's mother, Penny, smiled and sat down beside her.

'I'm sorry about your mother, Abbey. I know you would have liked to have her here today.'

'Thank you. I just wish my father could have made it over. It's too far, though, and I know he isn't strong enough at the moment.'

Penny touched her arm. 'You probably realise I am very proud of Darren and I just want to say I am so happy he has found you. I think you make a wonderful couple, and I'm thrilled for the pair of you.'

She gave Abbey a small ring box. Abbey opened it and inside was a diamond engagement ring.

'Darren's father gave me this ring when we got engaged. The diamond comes from one of the mines here. I think it is fitting that you have it now.'

She kissed Abbey on the cheek before walking away. Abbey felt the emotion beginning to well up inside her and knew that it soon would embellish itself into a flood of tears. She hastily walked over to the riverbank and looked towards the horizon. She took a deep breath and then let the tears fall. Tears of sadness mingled with tears of sheer joy. She looked up into the starry sky.

'I'm so sorry Mum, I really am. Be happy for me, please.'

Abbey had asked Boitachello to be her maid of honour. Phil, for once in his life, relented about wearing formal dress and agreed to wear a suit and walk Abbey down the aisle. Stuart, Darren's brother, was to be the best man. Mr Kobe and Mary organised the reception buffet, which was to be held in the Savuti Lodge gardens.

On the morning of the wedding, Darren left the bungalow early to change at the Hotel. Abbey sat on her bed looking at the dress, hanging up by the window. Mary and Abbey had flown to Johannesburg to buy the dress at Mary's insistence, who was determined that Abbey would not walk down the aisle in her cargo pants and Levi top.

The dress was a soft turquoise colour. Abbey had chosen it for its simple but classic style, trying to bring together the Abbey from England and the Abbey of Botswana, a combination that now resulted in a much wiser and contented woman.

A soft tapping on the bedroom door broke into her thoughts. She opened the door and found herself standing face to face with her father. Words escaped her momentarily and she clasped her hand over her mouth. Her father smiled and held out his hand. She suddenly regained control and hugged him warmly.

'You have chosen a very persistent man for your husband, Abbey,' he said, holding her close for the first time that she could ever remember.

Darren, not content with Abbey's disappointment at her father's initial refusal to come to the wedding, had telephoned him several times and eventually persuaded him to change his mind.

'I'll organise everything,' he had tried to reassure him. 'All you need to do is turn up at the airport and someone will assist you every step of the way.' Her father had flown in to Kasane on the first flight, and Abbey suddenly realised why Darren had left so early that morning.

At midday, Abbey walked down the aisle on the arm of the man she had secretly admired all her life. Apart from her mother's absence, the day was as perfect as she felt it could be. Phil, knowing full well that Abbey's father would be present at the wedding, had quickly changed his role to that of usher.

The whole town turned out to wish them well, joining in with the singing and dancing to the traditional wedding songs. The day seemed to fly by and, at times, Abbey felt as though she was a spectator in a dream. When Darren slipped the ring on her finger for a second time, she could hardly contain her excitement, waiting for the moment she could finally wrap her arms around him. Her newly acquired nephews, armed with cameras, captured the day's events, and Abbey made sure there were plenty of photographs to send home with her father. She hoped he would put one of them on the wall in the lounge, to show three generations of the Harris' family weddings.

That night, when all the celebrations had finished and the town had gone to sleep, Abbey woke her husband.

'What is it? Are you alright?' he asked, turning on the light.

'Come with me,' she said, pulling him out of bed.

'Where? Come with you where?' asked Darren, as he pulled on his jeans and shoes and followed Abbey out of the bungalow and down the drive. She led him by the hand into the President's Lodge and across to the pool.

She stripped in front of him.

'Going to join me or just going to watch?'

He took her into his arms. 'I've waited a long time for this particular dream to come true,' he said, before kicking off his shoes.

Epilogue

Darren and Abbey continued to live Kasane for the next five years and had three children. Abbey gave up her position with AVP after the birth of her second child and, despite her fears, she adapted into the role of being a mother quite easily, and consciously worked on building a good relationship with all her children.

When their eldest child turned four years old, they both decided that it was time to move on and introduce their children into a different culture. They sold their seventy per cent share of the safari business to Mr Kobe. It had been a resounding success, expanding across the country and into Namibia, making a substantial profit for the three partners.

Abbey's father visited Abbey on two more occasions after the wedding. She had watched him as he held his first grandchild with a look of complete adoration on his face. She had been right about one thing. It really is never too late! He died exactly three years to the day after her mother and, although Abbey didn't see him as often as she would have liked, they spoke regularly on the phone on a much deeper emotional level.

The death of her father left Abbey with an inheritance of half a million pounds. Financially secure from her inheritance and the sale of the business, Abbey and Darren Scott left Botswana and settled in Christchurch, South Island, New Zealand, living in the same district as Darren's brother and his family.

Phil decided to stay in Kasane and carried on working for AVP. He married Boitachello and, although they didn't have any children of their own, they adopted two local orphans. Phil became the football team coach and was known as an honorary Motswana in the town. As his daughter Lucy grew older, they communicated regularly by letter and e-mail and, by the time she was eight years old, she had started to call him Dad.

217

Mary Jenkins also stayed on in Kasane and married Mr Kobe. She had five blissful years with him before she was admitted to hospital with malaria and never recovered. She left seventy-five thousand pounds in her will to be used to build a new wing onto the hospital to accommodate patients with malaria and Aids. The ward was named after her. As per her wishes, she was buried in Kasane.

Mr Kobe sold the safari business to an American travel company one year after Abbey and Darren had left Kasane. He stayed on as manager of the Savuti Lodge Hotel until he retired on his fortieth birthday, when he realised a lifelong dream and went on a world tour. This was the first time he had ever travelled outside of Botswana.

Prisca died peacefully in her sleep, one month after her daughter's marriage. Abbey paid for the funeral and a small headstone in the town's graveyard.

Alfred left AVP and became the head gardener at the Savuti Lodge Hotel.

Isaac stayed at the Crossroads Café until he retired. By then, his application for citizenship had been approved, and he could end his days in the country he now felt very much a part of. He moved into a small house in Kasane where he spent his final years.

Mr Permelo was sentenced to ten years in prison for a number of offences. He opted to do his sentence in his native South Africa and was deported immediately.

Richard was never seen or heard of again.